£1-75

# JOURNEY BEYOND TOMORROW

Determined to see for himself the wonders of 21st-century
America, the prophet Joenes sets out from his Polynesian
island paradise. But from the moment he lays foot on US
soil, there is only one way his career can go – wrong.
Instantly embroiled in a series of bewildering events, he
finds himself hurtled from one misadventure to the next,
encountering, among others, the living dead of New York,
an electronic oracle and a psychotic policeman. For from
the horrors of its Utopia to the haven of its madhouses
21st-century America is a continent gone crazy...

Ebullient, provocative and above all, fun, *Journey Beyond
Tomorrow* is Sheckley's slickest satire.

ROBERT SHECKLEY ranks alongside Kurt Vonnegut as one
of science fiction's most respected satirists. Renowned as
much for his brilliant short stories as for his novels, he was
born in America in 1928, but has lived for long periods in
Europe.

GOLLANCZ CLASSIC SF

# ROBERT SHECKLEY

# JOURNEY BEYOND TOMORROW

VICTOR GOLLANCZ LTD
LONDON 1987

First published in Great Britain 1964
by Victor Gollancz Ltd
14 Henrietta Street, London WC2E 8QJ

First published in Gollancz Paperbacks 1987

An abridged version of *Journey Beyond Tomorrow*,
under the title *Journey of Joenes*, appeared in
*Fantasy & Science Fiction*

*British Library Cataloguing in Publication Data*
Sheckley, Robert
Journey beyond tomorrow.—(Gollancz classic
SF; no. 15).
I. Title
813'.54 [F]      PS3569.H392

ISBN 0-575-04122-6

Printed in Finland by Werner Söderström Oy

For Ziva, for Ruth Barnes, and
especially for Bill Barnes

# JOURNEY BEYOND TOMORROW

# INTRODUCTION

JOENES' fabulous world is more than a thousand years behind us, in the remote and misty past. We know that Joenes's Journey began around the year 2000, and ended in the opening years of our own era. We also know that the age through which Joenes travelled was remarkable for its industrial civilizations. Twenty-first-century mechanical articulation gave rise to many strange artifacts that no present-day reader has ever encountered. Still, most of us have learned at one time or another what the ancients meant by "guided missile," or "atom bomb." Fragments of some of these fantastic creations can be seen in many museums.

Our knowledge is much less certain of the customs and institutions by which men lived in the twenty-first century. And to discover anything at all about their religions and ethics, we must turn to Joenes's Journey.

Beyond a doubt, Joenes himself was an actual person; but there is no way of determining the authenticity of every story told about him. Some of the tales do not appear to be factual accounts, but rather, moral allegories. But even those that are considered allegorical are representative of the spirit and temper of the times.

Our book, then, is a collection of tales about the far-travelling Joenes and about his marvellous and tragic twenty-first century. A few of the tales are from written records. But most of them come to us through the oral tradition, handed down from storyteller to storyteller.

Aside from this book, the only written account of the Journey appears in the recently published *Fijian Tales,* where, for obvious reasons, Joenes's role is rendered as secondary to that of his friend Lum. This is quite untrue to the spirit of the Journey, and false to the content of the stories themselves. Because of this, we have felt the necessity of this book, in order that the entire body of Joenes Stories may be rendered faithfully in written form, to be preserved for future generations.

This volume also contains all of the twenty-first-century writing concerning Joenes. These written records are unfortunately few and fragmentary, and comprise only two of the stories. These are: "Lum's Meeting With Joenes," from the *Book of Fiji*, Orthodox Edition, and "How Lum Joined the Army," also from the *Book of Fiji*, Orthodox Edition.

All of the other stories are from the oral tradition, deriving from Joenes or his followers, and handed down from generation to generation. The present collection puts into written form the words of the most famous present-day storytellers, without any alteration in their various viewpoints, idiosyncrasies, moralities, style, comments, and so forth. We would like to thank those storytellers for graciously allowing us to put their words upon paper. These men are:

> Ma'aoa of Samoa
> Maubingi of Tahiti
> Paaui of Fiji
> Pelui of Easter Island
> Teleu of Huahine

We have used the particular tales or group of tales for which each of these men is most acclaimed. Credit is given at the beginning of each story. And we make our apologies to the many excellent storytellers we have been unable to include in this volume, and whose contributions will have to await the compilation of a Joenes *Variorum*.

For the reader's convenience these stories are arranged sequentially, as continuing chapters of an unfolding narrative, with a beginning, a middle, and an end. But the reader is warned not to expect a consistent and rationally ordered story, since some parts are long and some short, some complicated and some simple, depending upon the idiosyncrasy of the individual storyteller. Your editor could, of course, have taken from or added to the various parts, making their lengths regular and imposing his own sense of order and style upon the whole. But he thought it best to leave the tales as they were, in order to give the reader the entire unexpurgated Journey. This seemed only fair to the storytellers, and the only way to tell the whole truth about Joenes, the people he met, and the strange world he travelled through.

Your editor has taken down the exact words of the storytellers, and copied the two written accounts, but he himself has invented nothing, and has added no comments of his own to the tales. His only remarks are in the last chapter of the book, where he tells of the Journey's end.

Now, reader, we invite you to meet Joenes, and travel with him through the last years of the old world and the first years of the new.

# 1. JOENES BEGINS HIS JOURNEY

*(As told by Maubingi of Tahiti)*

IN the twenty-fifth year of his life, an event occurred that was of crucial significance to the hero of this tale. To explain the significance of this event, we must first tell something of our hero; and in order to understand our hero, something must be said of the place in which he lived, and of the condition and circumstances of that place. So we will begin there, moving as quickly as we can to the central matters this tale is actually about.

Our hero, Joenes, lived upon a small island in the Pacific Ocean, an atoll that lay 200 miles east of Tahiti. This island was called Manituatua, and it was no more than two miles long by several hundred yards in width. Surrounding it was a coral reef, and beyond the reef lay the blue waters of the Pacific. To this island Joenes's parents had come from America, to tend the equipment that supplied most of Eastern Polynesia with electrical power.

When Joenes's mother died, his father laboured alone; and when his father died, Joenes was requested by the Pacific Power Company to continue in his father's place. And this Joenes did.

By most accounts, Joenes was a tall, strongly built young man with a pleasing face and excellent manners. He was a great reader, and took delight in his father's extensive library. Since he was romantically inclined, his sensibilities led him towards the contemplation of truth, loyalty, love, duty, fate, chance, and other abstractions. Because of his temperament, Joenes saw virtues as mandates, and he loved to think of them in their most superlative form.

The people of Manituatua, all Polynesians from Tahiti, found it difficult to understand this sort of man. They readily admitted that virtue was good; but this did not prevent them from engaging in vice whenever necessary or convenient. Although Joenes scorned such behaviour, he could not help but be impressed by the good spirits, generosity, and easy sociability of the Manituatuans. Even though they rarely gave a thought to virtue, and even more rarely practised it, they managed somehow to lead pleasant and worthy lives.

This evidence did not immediately convert Joenes, who was still of too passionate a mentality to consider moderation. But it did have a constant and ever-growing effect upon him. Some say that Joenes's later survival was made possible only by the expediency he had learned from the Manituatuans.

But influences can only be guessed at, never truly delineated or understood. What we are leading up to is the great and singular event that came upon Joenes in his twenty-fifth year.

This event was formed in the executive office of the Pacific Power Company, situated in San Francisco, on the Western Coast of America. Here, potbellied men wearing suits, neckties, shirts, and shoes had gathered around a circular table made of gleaming teak. These Men of the Round Table, as they were called, held much of human destiny in their hands. Chairman of the Board was Arthur Pendragon, a man who had inherited his position but had been forced to wage a grim proxy fight before he could take his rightful place. Once established, Arthur Pendragon had fired the old Board of Trustees, and appointed his own men. Present were Bill Launcelot, a man of vast financial strength; Richard Galahad, well known for his charitable works; Austin Modred, who had political connections throughout the state; and many others.

These men, whose financial empire had been hard pressed of late, voted for a consolidation of their power and immediate disposition of all unprofitable holdings. This decision, simple as it seemed at the time, had far-reaching consequences.

In distant Manituatua, Joenes received word of the Board's decision to cease operation of the Eastern Polynesian power station.

Thus Joenes was out of a job. Worse still, he had lost an entire way of life.

During the next week, Joenes gave considerable thought to his future. His Polynesian friends urged him to stay with them on Manituatua; or, if he preferred, to go to one of the larger islands such as Huahine, Bora Bora, or Tahiti.

Joenes listened to their proposals, and then went to a private place to think. He emerged from this place after three days and announced to the waiting populace his intention of going to America, his parents' homeland, there to see with his own eyes the wonders about which he had read, to discover if his destiny lay there; and if not, to return to the people of Polynesia with a clear mind and open heart, ready to perform whatever services they required of him.

There was consternation among the people when they heard this, for the land of America was known to be more dangerous than the unpredictable ocean itself; and the Americans were reputed to be sorcerers and warlocks, who, through subtle enchantments, could change the entire way of a man's thinking. It seemed impossible that a man could grow to dislike coral beaches, lagoons, palm trees, outrigger canoes, and the like. Yet it had happened. Other men of Polynesia had journeyed to America, and had been exposed to the enchantments there, and had never returned. One had even visited legendary Madison Avenue; but what he found there is unknown, for that man never spoke again. Nevertheless, Joenes was determined to go.

Joenes was affianced to a Manituatuan girl of golden skin, almond eyes, black hair, a figure of the greatest piquancy, and a mind wise in the ways of men. Joenes proposed to send for this girl, whose name was Tondelayo, as soon as he had established himself in America; or, if fortune did not favour him, to return to her. Neither of these proposals met with Tondelayo's approval, and she spoke to Joenes in the following fashion, and in the local dialect then prevalent:

"Hey! you foolish popaa fella want one time go Melica? For why, hey? More coconut in Melica, maybe? Bigger beach? Better fishing? No! You think maybe better chumbi-chumbi, hey? I tell you no. More better you stay alongside here me one time, my word!"

In this fashion the lovely Tondelayo reasoned with Joenes. But Joenes answered:

"My darling, do you think it pleases me to leave *you*, the epitome of all my dreams and the crystallization of my desires? No, my darling, no! This departure fills me with dread, for I do not know what fate awaits me in the cold world to the east. I only know a man must go, must look at fame and fortune, and if need be, at death itself. For only in an understanding of the great world to the east, which I have heard of only through my departed parents and their books, can I ever return and spend my life here in these islands."

The lovely Tondelayo gave careful attention to these words, and pondered them long. And then the island girl spoke to Joenes the words of simple philosophy that had been passed down from mother to daughter from time immemorial:

"Hey, you fella white men all alike, I think. You chumbi-chumbi allatime little wahine okay, then you want walk-around look for chumbi-chumbi alongside popaa white woman American, I think. My word! And yet, the palm grows, the coral spreads, but man must die."

Joenes could only bow his head to the ancestral wisdom of the island girl. But his decision was not shaken. Joenes knew that it was his destiny to see the land of America from which his parents had come; there to accept whatever danger offered or danger proffered, and to come to terms with the unknowable fate that lies in ambush for all men. He kissed Tondelayo, who began crying when she saw that her words had no power to move this man.

The neighbouring chiefs gave a farewell feast for Joenes, at which they served island delicacies such as canned beef and canned pineapple. When the trading schooner touched at the island with the weekly supply of rum, they sadly bade their beloved Joenes farewell.

So it was that Joenes, with the melody of the islands ringing in his ears, made his way past Huahine and Bora Bora, past Tahiti and Hawaii, finally to arrive in the city of San Francisco upon the Western Coast of America.

## 2. LUM'S MEETING WITH JOENES

(*Lum's own words, as recorded in the* Book of Fiji, *Orthodox Edition*)

WELL I mean, you know how it is. It's like Hemingway said; the booze goes bad and the chick goes bad and where are you? So I was down at the docks waiting on the weekly shipment of peyote and I wasn't really doing anything, I was just standing around and digging it all—the people, the big ships, the Golden Gate, you know. I had just finished a sandwich made of Italian salami on real black pumpernickel bread, and what with the peyote coming, I wasn't feeling so bad. I mean sometimes you just don't feel so bad, you're out there digging it, even if the chick has gone bad.

This boat came in from one of those places and this guy got off. He was a tall, lean, sort of guy with a real-looking tan, a big set of shoulders on him, and he was wearing a shirt made of canvas and a pair of beat-up pants and no shoes at all. So naturally I thought he was OK. I mean he looked OK. So I came up to him and asked him if this was the boat the stuff had come in on.

This character looked at me, and he said, "My name's Joenes, I'm a stranger here."

So I knew at once he wasn't with it, and I just sort of stared away.

He said, "Do you know where I could find a job? I'm new in America, and I want to find out about it, and learn what America has for me, and what I have for America."

I started looking at him again because now I didn't know;

I mean it didn't look like he was with it, but not everyone is a hipster these days and sometimes the simple approach if you can make it work will take you all the way to the big Teahouse in the Sky run by the Biggest Pusher of Them All. I mean maybe he was playing it Zen with this what looked like cornball. Jesus was cornball, but he was with it, and all of us would be for him if only the squares would leave him alone. So I said to this Joenes, "You want a job? There anything you can do?"

Joenes said to me, "I can operate an electrical transformer."

"Goody for you," I told him.

"And play the guitar," he said.

"Well man," I said, "why didn't you say so in the first place instead of coming on so heavy with the electricity bit? I know a cappuccino place you can play, maybe get some tips from the squares. You got any bread, man?"

This Joenes barely spoke English, so I had to explain it all to him like I was drawing a blueprint. But he caught on pretty fast, about the guitar scene and the squares, and I offered him he could bunk for a while in my pad. I mean with my chick gone bad, why not? And this Joenes, he flashed me a smile and said sure, he'd go for that. And he asked me what the situation was locally, and aside from that, what we did for kicks. He sounded OK even if he was a foreigner, so I told him that chicks could be found, and that for kicks he'd better stick with me and look-see. He dug this so we went to the pad, where I gave him a sandwich of that real rye bread with the little seeds and a slab of Swiss cheese from Switzerland, not Wisconsin. Joenes was so far down I had to loan him my axe, on account he had left his own guitar in the islands, wherever the islands were. And that night we made the coffeehouse scene.

Well Joenes came on big that night with the guitar and

songs, because he sang in a language no one understood, which was just as well because the tunes were a little square. The tourists lapped it up like it was A.T. & T., and Joenes collected $8.30, which was enough for a nice big loaf of Russian rye and don't give me that unpatriotic bit, and some other stuff besides. And this little chick no more than 5′ 1″ latched on to him, because Joenes was that sort. I mean he was big and tall and he had shoulders like granddaddy's old ox yoke, and a big sweep of blond hair that was sun-streaked. A guy like me has more trouble, because even though I got a beard I'm built short and thick and sometimes it takes a while. But Joenes he was like magnetic. He even attracted the sunglasses, who asked him if he'd ever joypopped, but I pulled him off that, because the peyote had come and why trade a headache for an upset stomach?

So Joenes and this chick, who was named Deirdre Feinstein, and another chick she got for me, we all went back to the pad. I showed Joenes how you take the peyote buds and mash them down and so forth, and we all took it and we came on. I mean we came on, but Joenes lit up like a 1000-watt Mazda bulb and even though I warned him about the fuzz who are patrolling the streets and alleys of San Francisco these days looking for anybody who's on anything so they can use those beautiful new California jails of theirs, Joenes insisted on standing on the bed and making a speech. It was a pretty nice speech, because this big-shouldered laughing boy from the faraway hills was really turned on for the first time, and he put down The Word as follows:

" My friends, I have come to you from a faraway land of sand and palm upon a voyage of discovery, and I count myself fortunate above all men, for upon this my first night in your land I have been taken to your leader, King Peyote, and have been raised up instead of put down, and have been shown the wonders of the world which are presently turning red before me and falling like a waterfall. To my dear comrade, Lum, I can only praise without sufficiency this act of beatitude. To my new sweetheart, the luscious Deirdre Feinstein, let me tell you that I see a great flame growing within, and a high wind blowing without. To Lum's girl, whose name I unfortunately didn't catch, I say that I love you like a brother, incestuously, and yet with an innocence born of self-born innocence. And further——"

Well, this Joenes didn't have exactly a small voice. As a matter of fact, he sounded like a sea lion in rutting season, which is a sound none of you out there should miss. But it was too much for the pad, because the neighbours upstairs, who are square types that get up at 8:00 in the morning to do the bit, pounded on the ceiling and informed us this was one party too much and that they had informed the cops, by which they meant the fuzz.

Joenes and the girls were conked, but I pride myself on keeping a clear head for danger no matter what is drifting in my lungs or dancing in my veins. I wanted to flush the rest of the peyote, but Deirdre, who is so with it she sometimes scares you, insisted upon secreting the remaining buds in her maiden-form, where, she insisted, they would be safe from any harm. I got them all out of the pad, Joenes with my guitar clenched in his sunburned fist, and we got down none too soon, for a patrol car full of fuzz had just arrived. I cautioned the group to walk straight ahead like little soldiers because you can't play any games when you got stuff on you. But I hadn't counted on how far gone that Deirdre was.

We started walking and the cops came by and gave us coplike looks, and we kept on walking and the fuzz started passing remarks about beatniks and immorality and such. I tried to keep the group moving, but that Deirdre wouldn't

19

be called down. She turned on the fuzz and told them what she thought of them, which was a very unwise thing to do if you've got a vocabulary and a creative imagination like Deirdre has.

The top cop, a sergeant, said, "OK, sister, come with us. We're booking you, dig?"

And struggling and kicking, they pulled poor Deirdre towards the cop car. I could see Joenes's face setting itself in thoughtful, cop-hating lines, and I was afraid of trouble since filled with peyote as he was he loved Deirdre and indeed everybody except the fuzz.

I said to him, "Man, don't do a thing, this scene's gotta split and if Deirdre won't, she won't. I mean she's always fighting cops ever since she came out here from New York to study Zen, and she gets pulled in all the time so it's no big deal, especially since her father is Sean Feinstein who owns like anything you can name in five seconds. So the cops just sober her up and let her go. So don't make the move, man, don't even look back, because your father is not Sean Feinstein, or indeed anybody I ever heard of."

In this way I tried to soothe and reason with Joenes, but Joenes stopped, a heroic figure under the lamplight, his fist clenched white around my guitar, his eyes all-knowing and all-forgiving except for cops. And he turned.

The lead cop said, "You want something, kid?"

Joenes said, "Take your hands from off that young lady!"

The cop said, "This drug addict, whom you call a young lady, is in violation of section 431.3 of the Code of the City of San Francisco. I suggest that you mind your own business, buster, and don't play that ukelele on the streets after twelve o'clock"

I mean, he was being nice in his way.

But Joenes then made a speech which was a beauty, and I cannot recall it word for word, but the idea was that laws

20

are made by man and thus must partake of the evil nature of man, and that true morality lies in following the true dictates of the illuminated soul.

"A Commie, huh?" said the lead cop. And in a trice, or perhaps even sooner, they dragged Joenes into the cop car.

Well naturally Deirdre was sprung the following morning, on account of her father, and maybe also because of her winsome ways which are the talk of San Francisco. But though we searched high and low, and even as far afield as Berkeley, we saw no sign of Joenes.

No sign, I tell you! What had happened to this blond troubador with the sun-streaked hair and a heart as big as all outdoors when properly illuminated? Where had he gone, with my guitar (a genuine Tatay) and my second-best pair of sandals? I suppose only the cops know, and they will not tell. But still I remember him, Joenes the sweet singer, who, at the gates of hell, turned back to look for his Eurydice, and suffered thus the doom of Orpheus the golden-voiced. I mean it was a little different but still it was all there, and who knows in what distant lands Joenes and my guitar are wandering?

# 3. THE CONGRESSIONAL COMMITTEE

*(As told by Ma'aoa of Samoa)*

JOENES could not know that a committee of the American Senate was presently in San Francisco, carrying out investigations. But the police knew. They sensed intuitively that Joenes was a likely witness for these investigations, and they took him from the jail to the room where the Committee was meeting in executive session.

The Committee chairman, whose name was Senator George W. Pelops, immediately asked Joenes what he had to say for himself.

"I haven't done a thing," Joenes said.

"Ah," replied Pelops, "has anyone *accused* you of doing anything? Have I accused you? Have any of my illustrious colleagues? If so, I would like to hear of it at once."

"No sir," Joenes said. "I just thought——"

"Thoughts are not admissible as evidence," Pelops said.

Pelops then scratched his bald head, adjusted his spectacles, and glared full into a television camera. He said, "This man, by his own admission, has been accused of no crime whether of commission or omission. We have asked him here merely to talk, as is our congressional privilege and duty. And yet, his very words betray a consciousness of guilt. Gentlemen, I think we must pursue this a little further."

Joenes said, "I want a lawyer."

Pelops said, "You cannot have a lawyer, since this is only

a congressional fact-finding committee and not an arraignment. But we will take careful note of your request for one. Might I ask why a presumably innocent man might want a lawyer? "

Joenes, who had read many books on Manituatua, mumbled something about his rights and the law. Pelops told him that the Congress was the guardian of his rights, as well as the maker of the laws. Therefore he had nothing to fear if only he answered honestly. Joenes took heart at this and promised that he would answer honestly.

" I thank you for that," Pelops said, " although usually I do not have to *request* that a man answer honestly. Still, perhaps it means nothing. Tell me, Mr. Joenes, do you *believe* in the speech you made last night in the streets of San Francisco? "

" I don't remember any speech," said Joenes.

" You refuse to answer the question? "

" I can't answer it. I don't remember. I believe I was intoxicated."

" Do you remember who you were with last night? "

" I think I was with a man named Lum, and a girl named Deirdre——"

" We do not require their names," Pelops said hastily. " We simply asked you if you remembered who you were with, and you said you do so remember. I put it to you, Mr. Joenes, that it is a convenient memory which remembers one set of facts and forgets another, both occurring in the same period of twenty-four hours! "

" They weren't facts," Joenes said, " they were people."

" The Committee does not require you to be facetious," Pelops said sternly. " I will warn you here and now that facetious, unresponsive, or misleading answers, as well as no answers at all, can be interpreted as contempt of Congress, which is a federal offence punishable by up to a year in prison."

23

"I didn't mean anything," Joenes said quickly.

"Very well, Mr. Joenes, we will continue. Do you deny that you made a speech last night?"

"No sir, I don't deny it."

"And do you deny that the content of your speech concerned the so-called right which you insisted every man had to overthrow the legally constituted law of this land? Or, to put it in another way, do you deny that you incited to rebellion those dissidents who might be swayed by your foreign-inspired words? Or, to make the matter perfectly plain to you, that you advocated violent overthrow of the government which necessarily rests upon the laws *of* that government? Can you argue that the sum and content of your speech was a violation of those liberties which our Founding Fathers gave us, and which allow such as you to speak at all, as you surely would *not* be allowed to do in Soviet Russia? Will you presume to tell us that this speech, masked under the garb of harmless bohemianism, was not part of a detailed plot directed towards inner dissension and for the purpose of paving the way for outer aggression, and that in this attempt you had the silent approval, if not the explicit direction, of certain persons in our own State Department? And that, finally, this speech, which you disguised under an apparent intoxication, and which you gave under your presumed right to act subversively in a democracy where the power to retaliate, or so you thought, is hamstrung by a Constitution and a Bill of Rights which however is not, as you might think, designed to aid the lawless, but rather to preserve the liberties of the people against godless mercenaries such as yourself? Did you or did you not, Mr. Joenes? I ask only a simple yes or no."

"Well," Joenes said, "I'd like to clarify——"

"The question, Mr. Joenes," said Pelops in an icy voice. "Kindly answer the question yes or no."

Joenes racked his brain furiously, remembering all the American history he had read upon his native island. Now he said, "The allegation is monstrous!"

"Answer the question, Mr. Joenes," Pelops said.

Joenes said, "I stand upon my Constitutional rights, namely the First and Fifth Amendments, and respectfully decline to answer."

Pelops smiled thinly. "You may not do so, Mr. Joenes, since the Constitution to which you *now* so fervently cling has been reinterpreted, or rather brought up to date, by those of us who wish to preserve it from change and desecration. The Amendments you mention, Mr. Joenes—or should I say Comrade Joenes—will not permit you to be silent for reasons which any judge of the Supreme Court would have been glad to tell you—*had you chosen to ask him!*"

There was no answer to this crushing rejoinder. Even the reporters in the room, hardened observers of the political scene, were moved. Joenes turned beet-red and then lily-white. With no recourse left, he opened his mouth to answer. But he was momentarily saved by the intervention of one of the members of the Committee, Senator Trellid.

"Excuse me, sir," Senator Trellid said to Pelops, "and excuse me all of you who are waiting for this man's answer. I just want to say one thing, and I want it to go on the record, because sometimes a man must speak out no matter how painful it is to him, and in spite of that it might harm him politically and economically. And yet, it is the duty of a man such as myself to speak out when he must, and to speak in spite of consequences, and in full conscience, even if what he has to say goes against the great power of public opinion. Therefore I want to say this, I am an old man, and I have seen many things in my time, and I have witnessed even more. Perhaps I am not wise to so speak, but I must tell you that I am dead set against injustice. Unlike some, I cannot condone the slaughter of the Hungarians, the unlawful seizure of China, nor the communization of Cuba. I am old, I have been called conservative, but I cannot condone these things. And, no matter who calls me what, I hope I will never live to see the day when a Russian army occupies the city of Washington, D.C. Thus I speak against this man, this Comrade Jonski, not as a senator, but rather as one who was once a child in the hill country south of Sour Mountain, who fished and hunted in the deep woods, who grew slowly to an awareness of what America meant to him, whose neighbours sent him to Congress to represent them and their dear ones, and who now feels called upon to make this declaration of faith. It is for this reason and this reason only that I say to you in the words of the Bible, 'Evil is Bad!' Some of the sophisticated among us may laugh at this, but there it is and I believe it."

The Committee burst into spontaneous applause at the old senator's speech. Although they had heard it many times, it never failed to elicit in them emotions of the deepest and most exquisite sort. Now, white-lipped, Chairman Pelops turned to Joenes.

"Comrade," he asked, with simple irony, "are you at this present time a card-carrying member of the Communist Party?"

"I am not!" cried Joenes.

Pelops said, "In that case, who were your associates during your card-carrying days?"

"I didn't have any associates. I mean——"

"We understand very well what you mean," Pelops said. "Since you choose not to identify your fellow traitors, would you mind telling us the location of your cell? No? Tell me, Comrade Jonski, does the name Ronald Black mean anything to you? Or to put it more simply, when did you last see Ronald Black?"

"I never met him," Joenes said.

"Never? That is a very big word, Mr. Joenes. Are you trying to tell me that at no time could you have met Ronald Black? That you might not have *innocently* passed this man in a crowd, or perhaps attended a movie with him? I doubt if any man in America can so flatly state that he has *never* met Ronald Black. Do you wish your statement to go on the record?"

"Well, I mean, I might have met him in a crowd, I mean been in a crowd where he was, but I don't know for sure——"

"But you allow the possibility?"

"I guess so."

"Excellent," Pelops said. "Now we are getting somewhere. Now I ask you what crowd you met Black in, and what he said to you, and you to him, and what papers he passed you, and whom you passed those papers to——"

"I never met Arnold Black!" Joenes cried.

"We have always known him as *Ronald* Black," Pelops said. "But we are always glad to learn his pseudonyms. Note please that you yourself admitted the possibility of your association with him, and in view of your admitted Party activities, this possibility must be judged a probability so strong as to be a certainty. Furthermore, you yourself gave us the name by which Ronald Black was known in the Party, a name which we hitherto *had not known*. And that, I think, is sufficient."

"Look," said Joenes, "I don't know this Black or what he did."

In sombre tones Pelops stated, "Ronald Black was convicted of stealing the plans for the new Studebaker Roadclinger Super V-12 Luxury Compact Convertible, and selling those plans to an agent of the Soviet Union. After a fair trial, Black was executed in the manner prescribed by the law. Later, thirty-one of his associates were discovered,

27

tried, and executed. You, Comrade Jonski, will be associate Number 32 in the biggest spy ring we have yet uncovered."

Joenes tried to speak, but found himself speechless and trembling in fear.

"This Committee," Pelops summed up, "has been granted extralegal powers because it is merely investigative, not punitive. This is perhaps a shame, but the letter of the law must be followed. Therefore we now hand the secret agent Jonski over to the office of the Attorney General, there to undergo fair trial by due process of law, and to suffer whatever punishment that branch of the government deems fitting for a self-admitted traitor who deserves only death. This meeting is now adjourned."

In this fashion, Joenes was swiftly transferred to the punitive branch of the government and bound over to the Attorney General.

# 4. HOW JOENES WAS GIVEN JUSTICE

*(As told by Pelui of Easter Island)*

THE Attorney General, to whom Joenes was bound over, was a tall man with a hawk face, narrow eyes, bloodless lips, and a face that looked as though it had been hammered out of raw iron. Stooped and silently contemptuous, startling in his black velvet cloak and ruffled collar, the Attorney General was the living embodiment of his terrible office. Since he was a servant of the punitive branch of the government, his duty was to call down retribution upon all who fell into his hands, and to do so by any means in his power.

The Attorney General's place of residence was Washington. But he himself was a citizen of Athens, New York, and in his youth had been an acquaintance of Aristotle and Alcibiades, whose writings are the distillation of American genius.

Athens was one of the cities of ancient Hellas, from which the American civilization had sprung. Near Athens was Sparta, a military power that had held leadership over the Lacedaemonian cities of upper New York State. Ionian Athens and Dorian Sparta had fought a disastrous war, and had lost their independence to American rule. But they were still influential in the politics of America, especially since Washington had been the seat of Hellenic power.

At first, the case of Joenes seemed simple enough. Joenes had no important friends or political colleagues, and it seemed that retribution might be visited upon him with impunity. Accordingly, the Attorney General arranged for Joenes to receive every possible sort of legal advice, and then to be tried by a jury of his peers in the famous Star Chamber. In this way the exact letter of the law would be carried out, but with a comforting foreknowledge of the verdict the jury would render. For the punctilious jurors of the Star Chamber, utterly dedicated to the eradication of any vestige of evil, had never in their history given any verdict but guilty.

After the verdict should be delivered, the Attorney General planned to sacrifice Joenes upon the Electric Chair at Delphi, thus winning favour in the eyes of gods and men.

This was his plan. But further investigation showed that Joenes's father had been a Dorian from Mechanicsville, New York, and a magistrate of that community. And Joenes's mother had been an Ionian from Miami, an Athenian colony deep in Barbarian territory. Because of this, certain influential Hellenes urged mercy for the erring son of respectable parents, and for the sake of Hellenic unity, which was a force to be reckoned with in American politics.

The Attorney General, an Athenian himself, thought it best to comply with this request. Therefore he dissolved the Star Chamber and sent Joenes to the great Oracle at Sperry. This met with approval, for the Sperry Oracle, like the Oracles at Genmotor and Genelectric, was known to be absolutely fair and impartial in its judgments of men and their actions. In fact, the Oracles gave such good justice that they had replaced many of the courts of the land.

Joenes was brought to Sperry and was told to stand before the Oracle. This he did, although his knees were shaking. The Oracle was a great calculating machine of the most complex variety, with a switchboard, or altar, attended by many priests. These priests had been castrated so they should think no thoughts except of the machine. And the high priest had been blinded also, so that he could see penitents only through the eyes of the Oracle.

When the high priest entered, Joenes prostrated himself before him. But the priest raised him up and said, "My son, fear not. Death is the common destiny of all men, and ceaseless travail is their condition throughout the ephemeral life of the senses. Tell me, do you have any money?"

Joenes said, "I have eight dollars and thirty cents. But why do you ask, Father?"

"Because," the high priest said, "it is common practice for the supplicants to make voluntary sacrifice of money to the Oracle. But if you do not have the money, you can give equally acceptable things such as chattel mortgages, bonds, stocks, deeds, or any other papers which men deem of value."

"I have none of these things," Joenes said sadly.

"Do you not own lands in Polynesia?" the priest asked.

"I do not," Joenes said. "My parents' land was given to them by the government, to whom it must return. Nor do I hold other properties, for in Polynesia such things are not considered important."

"Then you own nothing?" the priest asked. He seemed disturbed.

"Nothing but eight dollars and thirty cents," Joenes said, "and a guitar which is not my own but belongs to a man named Lum in distant California. But Father, are these things really necessary?"

"Of course not," the priest replied. "But even cyberneticists must live, and an act of generosity from a stranger is looked upon as pleasing, especially when the time comes to interpret the words of the Oracle. Also, some believe that a penniless man is one who has not worked to amass money for the Oracle in case the day of divine wrath should ever be upon him, and who is therefore lacking in piety. But that need not concern us. We will now state your case, and ask for a judgment."

The priest took the Attorney General's statement, and Joenes's defence, and translated them into the secret language in which the Oracle listened to the words of men. Soon there was a reply.

The Oracle's judgment was as follows:

SQUARE IT TO THE TENTH POWER MINUS THE SQUARE ROOT OF MINUS ONE.

DO NOT FORGET THE COSINE, FOR MEN MUST NEEDS HAVE FUN.

ADD IN X AS A VARIABLE, FREE-FLOATING, FANCY-FREE.

IT WILL COME AT LAST TO ZERO, AND MORE YOU NEED NOT ME.

When this decision had been delivered, the priests met to interpret the words of the Oracle. And this is what they said:

SQUARE IT means correct the wrong.

THE TENTH POWER is the degree and number in which the penitent must labour in penal servitude in order to correct the wrong; namely ten years.

THE SQUARE ROOT OF MINUS ONE, being an imaginary number, represents a fictitious state of grace; but being instrumental, represents also the possibility of power and fame for the supplicant. Because of this, the previous ten-year sentence is suspended.

THE X VARIABLE represents the incarnate furies of the earth, among whom the supplicant shall dwell, and who shall show him all possible horrors.

THE COSINE is the mark of the goddess herself, protecting the supplicant from some of the terror of the furies, and promising him certain fleshly joys.

IT WILL COME AT LAST TO ZERO, means that the equation of divine justice and human guilt is balanced in this case.

MORE YOU NEED NOT ME, means that the supplicant may not apply again to this or any other Oracle, since the rendering is complete.

So it was that Joenes received a ten-year suspended sentence. And the Attorney General had to obey the decision of the Oracle and set him free.

Once freed, Joenes continued his journey through the land of America, bearing upon his head a curse and a promise, as well as a ten-year suspended sentence. He departed hastily from Sperry and rode a train to the great city of New York. And what he did there, and what happened to him, is the story which must now be told.

## 5. THE STORY OF JOENES, WATTS, AND THE POLICEMAN

### (As told by Ma'aoa of Samoa)

NEVER had Joenes seen anything like the great city of New York. The ceaseless rush and bustle of so many people was strange to him, but curiously exciting. When night came, the frantic life of the city continued unabated, and Joenes observed New Yorkers hurrying in and out of night-clubs and dance halls in their quest for pleasure. Nor was there any lack of culture in the city, for great numbers of people were attentive to the lost art of the moving pictures.

In the small hours of the night, the city's pace slowed. Then Joenes came upon many old men, and some young ones too, who sat listlessly on benches or stood near subway exits. When Joenes looked into their faces he saw a terrible nothingness, and when he spoke to them he could not understand their mumbled replies. These atypical New Yorkers disturbed him, and Joenes was glad when morning came.

At first light, the frenzied movements of the crowds began again, and people pushed and shoved each other in their haste to get somewhere and do something. Joenes wanted to learn the reason for all of this, so he chose a man out of the crowd and stopped him.

"Sir," Joenes said, "could you spare a moment of your valuable time and tell a stranger something about the great and purposeful vitality I see all around me?"

The man said, "Whatsamatter, you some kind of nut?" And he hurried off.

But the next man Joenes stopped gave the question careful thought, and said, "You call it vitality, huh?"

"So it appears," Joenes said, glancing at the restless crowds surging around them. "By the way, my name is Joenes."

"Mine's Watts," the man said, "as in Watts the matter. In answer to your question, I'll tell you that what you see is not vitality. It's panic."

"But what are they in a panic about?" Joenes asked.

"To put it in a nutshell," Watts said, "they're afraid if they stop hurrying and pushing, somebody will find out they're dead. It's a very serious matter being found dead, because then they can fire you from your job, foreclose all your bills, raise your apartment rental, and carry you squirming to your grave."

Joenes found this reply scarcely credible. He said, "Mr. Watts, these people do not look dead. And in actual fact, all exaggeration aside, they are *not* dead, are they?"

"I never put exaggeration aside," Watts told him. "But since you're a stranger, I'll try to explain a little more. To begin with, death is merely a matter of definition. Once the definition was very simple: you were dead when you stopped moving for a long time. But now the scientists have examined this antiquated notion more carefully, and have done considerable research on the entire subject. They have found that you can be dead in all important respects, but still go on walking and talking."

"What are these important respects?" Joenes asked.

"First of all," Watts told him, "the walking dead are characterized by an almost total lack of emotionality. They can feel only anger and fear, though they sometimes simulate other emotions in the crude manner of a chimpanzee pretending to read a book. Next, there is a robotic quality in their actions, which accompanies a cessation of the higher thinking processes. Frequently there is a reflex motion toward piety, which is not unlike the frantic movements that a chicken makes after its head has been chopped off. Because of this reflex, many of the walking dead are detected around churches, where some of them even try to pray. Others can be found on park benches or near subway exits——"

"Ah," said Joenes. "When I walked in the city late last night I saw certain men at those places——"

"Exactly," said Watts. "Those are the ones who no longer pretend that they are not dead. But others copy the living with great and pathetic earnestness, hoping to pass unnoticed. They can usually be detected because they overdo it, either by talking too much or by laughing too hard."

"I had no idea of all this," Joenes said.

"It is a tragic problem," Watts said. "The authorities are doing their best to cope with it, but it has assumed formidable proportions. I wish I could tell you other characteristics of the walking dead, and how they resemble the old-fashioned nonwalking dead, for I'm sure that you would find it interesting. But now, Mr. Joenes, I see a policeman approaching, and therefore I had better make my departure."

So saying, Watts broke into a full sprint and raced through the crowd. The policeman started after him, but soon gave up the pursuit and returned to Joenes.

"Damn it," the policeman said, "I've lost him again."

"Is he a criminal?" Joenes asked.

"Smartest jewel thief in these parts," the policeman said, mopping his massive red brow. "He likes to disguise himself as a beatnik."

"He was talking to me about the walking dead," Joenes said.

"He's always making up those stories," the policeman told him. "Compulsive liar, that's what he is. Crazy. And dangerous as they come. Especially dangerous because he doesn't carry a gun. I've almost caught him three times. I order him to stop in the name of the law, just like the book says, and when he doesn't stop, I shoot at him. So far I've killed eight bystanders. The way I'm going, I'll probably

36

never make sergeant. They make me pay for my own bullets, too."

"But if this Watts never carries a gun—" Joenes began, then stopped abruptly. He had seen a strange sullen expression cross the policeman's face, and had seen his hand drop to the butt of his gun. "What I meant to say," Joenes continued, "is there anything in what Watts told me about the walking dead?"

"Naw, that's just a beatnik line he makes up to kid people with. Didn't I tell you he was a jewel thief?"

"I forgot," Joenes said.

"Well don't forget it. I'm just a plain ordinary man, but a guy like Watts gets me sore. I do my duty just like the book says, and in the evening I go home and watch the TV, except on Friday evenings when I go bowling. Does that sound like being a robot, like Watts says?"

"Of course not," Joenes said.

"That guy," the policeman continued, "talks about people not having no emotion. Let me tell you, I'm maybe no psychologist, but I know I got emotions. When I have this gun in my hand, I feel good. Does that sound like I got no emotions? Furthermore, let me tell you something. I was raised in a tough section of this city, and when I was a kid I used to run with a gang. We all had zip guns and gravity knives, and we enjoyed ourselves with armed robbery, murder, and rape. Does that sound like no emotion? And I might of gone right on in that way, from being a kid criminal to being an adult criminal, if I hadn't met this priest. He wasn't no stuffed shirt, he was just like one of us, because he knew that was the only way he could reach us wild types. He used to go out on stomps with us, and more than once I saw him cut the hell out of somebody with a little switchblade he always carried. So he was regular and we accepted him. But he was also a priest, and seeing he was regular I let him talk to me.

37

And he told me how I was wasting my life in that way."

"He must have been a wonderful man," Joenes said.

"He was a saint," the policeman said, in a heavy brooding voice. "That man was a real saint, because he did everything we did but he was good inside and he always told us we should get out of criminality."

The policeman looked Joenes in the eye and said, "Because of that man, I became a cop. Me, who everyone thought would end up in the electric chair! And that Watts has the nerve to speak of the walking dead. I became a cop, and I've been a good cop instead of some lousy punk hoodlum like Watts. I've killed eight criminals in the line of duty, winning three merit badges from the department. And I've also accidentally killed twenty-seven innocent bystanders who didn't get out of the way fast enough. I'm sorry about those people, but I've got a job to do, and I can't let people get in the way when I'm going after a criminal. And no matter what the newspapers say, I've never taken a bribe in my life, not even for a parking ticket." The policeman's hand tightened convulsively around the butt of his revolver. "I'd give a parking ticket to Jesus Christ himself and no number of saints would be able to bribe me. What do you think about that?"

"I think you are a dedicated man," Joenes said carefully.

"You're right. And I've got a beautiful wife and three wonderful children. I've taught them all how to shoot a revolver. Nothing's too good for my family. And Watts thinks he knows something about emotion! Christ, these smooth-talking bastards get me so sore sometimes I can feel my head coming off. It's a good thing I'm a religious man."

"I'm sure it is," Joenes said.

"I still go every week to see that priest who got me out of the gang. He's still working with kids, because he's dedicated. He's getting sorta old to use a knife, so now it's usually a zip gun, or sometimes a bicycle chain. That man has done more for the cause of law than all the youth rehabilitation centres in the city. I give him a hand sometimes, and between us we've redeemed fourteen boys who you would have thought were hopeless criminals. Many of them are respected businessmen now, and six have joined the police force. Whenever I see that old man, I *feel* religion."

"I think that's wonderful," Joenes said. He began backing away, because the policeman had drawn his revolver and was toying with it nervously.

"There's nothing wrong with this country that good-heartedness and straight thinking won't cure," the policeman said, his jaw twitching. "Good always triumphs in the end, and it always will as long as there are good-hearted men to help it along. There's more law in the end of my nightstick than in all the musty old lawbooks. We bring them in and the judges let them go. What about that? Nice state of business, huh? But us cops are used to it, and we figure one broken arm is worth a year in stir, so we take care of a lot of the sentencing ourselves."

Here the policeman drew his nightstick. With it in one hand, his revolver in the other, he looked hard at Joenes. Joenes sensed the sudden hugeness of the policeman's need to enforce law and order. He stood utterly still, hoping that the policeman, now advancing towards him with shining eyes, would not kill him or break any bones.

A crucial moment was approaching. But Joenes was saved at the last moment by a citizen of the city, who, made absentminded by the tropic sun, stepped off the kerb before the traffic light changed to green.

The policeman whirled, fired two warning shots, and charged towards the man. Joenes walked quickly away in the opposite direction until he was beyond the limits of the city.

# 6. JOENES AND THE THREE TRUCK DRIVERS

*(This and the three Truck Driver stories that comprise it are told by Teleu of Huahine)*

As Joenes was walking along a highway to the north, a truck stopped beside him. Within the truck were three men who said they would willingly give him a ride as far as they were going.

Very happily Joenes got into the truck, declaring his gratitude to the truck drivers. But they said the pleasure was theirs, since driving a truck was lonely work even for three, and they enjoyed talking to different men and hearing of their adventures. This being the case, they asked Joenes to tell what had happened to him since he had left his home.

Joenes told these men that he was from a distant island, had come to the city of San Francisco where he had been arrested, questioned before a Congressional Committee, tried by an Oracle and given a ten-year suspended sentence, gone to New York where a policeman had nearly killed him. Nothing had gone right since he had left his island, Joenes said, and everything had gone badly. Therefore he considered himself a very unfortunate man.

"Mr. Joenes," said the first truck driver, "you have indeed gone through misfortunes. But I am the most unfortunate of men, for I have lost something more precious than gold, the loss of which I bemoan every day of my life."

Joenes asked the man to tell his story. And this is the story that the first truck driver told.

## THE STORY OF THE
## SCIENTIFIC TRUCK DRIVER

My name is Adolphus Proponus, and by birth I am a Swede. Ever since I was a child, I loved science. I possessed that love not merely for itself, but because I believed that science was mankind's greatest servant, which would lift humanity out of the cruelty of the past, to peace and happiness. In spite of all the atrocities I saw men perform, and even though my own neutral country grew rich by supplying guns to warring nations, I still believed in the goodness and superiority of mankind, and in its liberation through science.

Because of my humanistic instincts and my scientific inclinations, I became a doctor. I applied for work at the United Nations Health Commission, desiring the furthest and most wretched place on earth for my post. Not for me a quiet practice in a somnolent Swedish town; I wished to throw myself deep into the battle against disease, and for humanity.

I was sent to a place on the coast of Western Africa, there to be the sole doctor for an area larger than Europe. I was replacing a man named Durr, a Swiss who had died of the bite of a horned viper.

This area obviously needed a good doctor, since there was a great prevalence of diseases. Many of these were known to me, for I had studied them in books. Others were new. The new ones, I learned, had been propagated artificially, as part of the neutralization of Africa. I do not know whose decision this was, but someone had wished a truly neutral Africa, which could assist neither East nor

West. To this purpose germs had been introduced, and also certain laboratory plants, which had the effect of making dense jungle even denser. These things stopped men from having time for politics, since all their time had to be spent in a battle for life itself.

These things had also wiped out several hundred million Western troops, who were engaged in combat against Eastern guerrillas. The guerrillas, too, were wiped out. Also many species of animal had been destroyed, although a few had thrived. The rat, for example, flourished. Snakes of all species multiplied. Among insects, there was a great increase in flies and mosquitoes. Among birds, the vultures had increased beyond counting.

I had never known about this state of affairs, since news like this is generally ignored in a democracy, and is banned in a dictatorship. But I saw these horrors in Africa. And I learned that the same was true in the tropical parts of Asia, Central America, and India. All of those places were now truly neutral, through accident or through design, since they were engaged in a desperate struggle for life itself.

As a doctor I was saddened because of the many diseases, old and new. These sprang from the jungle, which had been aided and augmented by man. The growth rate of that jungle was fantastic; and therefore equally fantastic was its decay rate. Because of this, disease germs of all kinds multiplied and spread in the most congenial atmosphere possible.

As a man I was maddened by the perverted way in which science had been used. But still I believed in science. I told myself that evil men of little vision had created much harm in the world; but that humanitarians, working through science, would set it all right again.

I set to work with a will, aided by humanitarians the world over. I went to all the tribes within my district, treating their illnesses with my supplies of drugs. My successes were overwhelming.

But then the spawning diseases became resistant to my drugs, and new epidemics began. The tribes, although strong in their resistance, suffered terribly.

I wired urgently for newer drugs. These were sent to me, and I put down the epidemic. But a few of the germs and viruses managed to survive, and disease spread once again.

I requested newer drugs, and these were also sent to me. Once again disease and I were locked in mortal combat, from which I emerged victorious. But there were always a few organisms that escaped my drugs. Also, there were mutations to be reckoned with. Given the right environment, I learned that diseases could change into new and virulent forms much faster than men could make or discover new drugs.

In fact, I found that germs behaved quite like humans in times of stress. They showed every evidence of an astonishing will to survive; and quite naturally, the harder one struck at them, the faster and more frantically they spawned, mutated, resisted, and at last, struck back. The resemblance was, to my way of thinking, uncanny and unnatural.

I was labouring prodigiously at the time, twelve to eighteen hours a day, trying to save the poor, patient, suffering population. But disease outstripped my latest drugs, won a sort of victory, and raged with unbelievable violence. I was in despair, for no new drugs had been invented to meet these newest ills.

Then I found that the germs, in mutating to meet my new drugs, had become vulnerable once again to the old drugs. Therefore, in a perfect frenzy of scientific fervour, I began to apply the old drugs once more.

Since I had come to Africa, I had battled no less than ten major epidemics. Now I was beginning to fight my eleventh. And I knew that the germs and viruses would retreat before my attack, spawn, mutate, and strike again, leaving me to fight a twelfth epidemic, with similar results, and then a thirteenth, and so forth.

This was the situation into which my scientific and humanistic zeal had carried me. But I was drunk with fatigue, and half dead with my labours. I had no time to think of anything but the immediate problem.

But then the people of my district took the problem out of my hands. They possessed very little education, and they saw only the great epidemics which had ravaged them since my coming. Those people looked upon me as a sort of supremely evil witch doctor, whose bottles of supposed healing drugs actually contained the refined essences of the diseases that had ravaged them. They turned to their own witch doctors, who treated the sick with useless daubs of mud and bits of bone, and blamed every death upon some innocent tribesman.

Even the mothers whose children I had saved now turned against me. These mothers pointed out that the children had died anyhow, of starvation instead of disease.

At last the men of the villages gathered to kill me. They would have done so if I had not been saved by the witch doctors. This was an irony, because I considered the witch doctors my greatest antagonists.

The witch doctors explained to the people that if I were killed, a fiend of even greater evil power would be sent to them. Therefore the people did me no harm; and the witch doctors grinned at me, because they considered me a colleague.

Still I would not abandon my work among the tribes. For that reason, the tribes abandoned me. They moved inland to an area of desolate swamp, where food was scarce and disease was common.

I could not follow them, since the swamp was in a

different district. This district had its own doctor, also a Swede, who gave out no drugs at all, no pills, no injections, nothing. Instead, he got drunk every day on his own supplies of alcohol. He had lived in the jungle for twenty years, and he said he knew what was best.

Left completely alone in my district, I had a nervous collapse. I was sent back to Sweden, and there I thought about everything that had happened.

It seemed to me that the villagers and witch doctors, whom I had considered so perversely intractable, had merely behaved with good common sense. They had fled from my science and my humanism, which had improved their lot not an iota. On the contrary, my science had done nothing but produce more pain and suffering for them, and my humanism had foolishly attempted to wipe out other creatures for their benefit, and by doing so had upset the balance of forces upon the Earth.

Realizing all this, I fled my country, fled Europe itself, and came here. Now I drive a truck. And when someome speaks to me in glowing words about science and humanity and the marvels of healing, I stare at him as though he were insane.

That is how I lost my belief in science, a thing more precious to me than gold, the loss of which I bemoan every day of my life.

At the end of this story, the second truck driver said, "No one would deny that you had misfortunes, Joenes, But these are less than what my friend has just told you. And my friend's misfortunes are less than mine. For I am the most unfortunate of men, and I have lost something more precious than gold and more valuable than science, the loss of which I bemoan every day of my life."

Joenes asked the man to tell his story. And this is the story the second truck driver told.

My name is Ramon Delgado, and I am from the land of Mexico. My one great pride was in being an honest man. I was honest because of the laws of the land, which told me to be so, and which had been written by the best of men, who had derived them from universally accepted principles of justice, and had fortified them with punishments so that all men, not just those of goodwill, would obey.

This seemed right to me, because I loved justice and believed in it, and therefore believed in the laws that were derived from justice, and in the punishment that enforced the law. Not only did I feel that man's conception and execution of justice was good; I also felt that it was necessary. For only through this could there be freedom from tyranny and a sense of personal dignity.

I laboured for many years in my village, saved my money, and led an honest and upright life. One day I was offered a job in the capital. I was very happy about this, for I had long desired to see that great city from which the justice of my country derives.

I used all my savings to purchase an old automobile, and I drove to the capital. I parked in front of my new employer's store, where I found a parking meter. I went inside the store in order to get a peso to put in the parking meter. When I came out, I was arrested.

I was taken before a judge who accused me of illegal parking, petty larceny, vagrancy, resisting arrest, and creating a public disturbance.

The judge found me guilty of all these things. Of illegal parking, because there had been no money in the meter; petty larcency, because I had taken a peso from my employer's till to put in the meter; vagrancy, because I had

46

had only a single peso on my person; resisting arrest, because I had argued with the policeman; and creating a public disturbance, because I had wept when he took me to the jail.

In a technical sense, all these things were true, so I considered it no miscarriage of justice when the judge found me guilty. In fact, I admired his zeal in serving the law.

Nor did I complain when he sentenced me to ten years of imprisonment. This seemed severe, but I knew that the law could be upheld only through stern and uncompromising punishment.

I was sent to the Federal Penitentiary of Morelos, and I knew that it would be good for me to see the place where punishment is served out, and thus to learn the bitter fruits of dishonesty.

When I arrived at the Penitentiary, I saw a crowd of men hiding in the woods nearby. I took no notice of them, for the guard at the gate was reading my commitment papers. He studied them with great care, then opened the gate.

As soon as the gate was open, I was amazed to see that crowd of men come out of hiding, rush forward, and force their way into the prison. Many guards came out and tried to push the men back. Nevertheless, some were able to get into the Penitentiary before the admittance guard was finally able to close the gate.

"Is it possible," I asked him, "that those men wanted to get into prison on purpose?'

"Obviously they did," the guard said.

"But I had always thought that prisons were for the purpose of keeping people in rather than out," I said.

"They used to be," the guard told me. "But nowadays, with so many foreigners in the country, and so much starvation, men break into prison merely to get three meals a day. There's nothing we can do about it. By breaking

47

into prison they become criminals, and we have to let them stay."

"Disgraceful!" I said. "But what do the foreigners have to do with it?"

"They started all the trouble," the guard said. "There's starvation in their own countries, and they know that we in Mexico have the world's best prisons. So they come great distances in order to break into our prisons, especially when they can't break into their own. But I suppose foreigners are really no worse or better than our own people, who do the same thing."

"If this is the case," I said, "how can the government enforce its laws?"

"Only by keeping the truth a secret," the guard told me. "Someday we will be able to build penitentiaries that will keep the right people in and the wrong ones out. But until that time comes, the thing must be kept secret. In that way, most of the population still believes they should fear punishment."

The guard then escorted me inside the Penitentiary, to the office of the Parole Board. There a man asked me how I liked prison life. I told him that I wasn't sure yet.

"Well," the man said, "your behaviour for the entire time you have been here has been exemplary. Reform is our motive, not revenge. Would you like an immediate parole?"

I was afraid of saying the wrong thing, so I told him I wasn't sure.

"Take your time," he said, "and return to this office any time you want to be released."

Then I went to my cell. Within I found two Mexicans and three foreigners. One of the foreigners was an American, and the other two were Frenchmen. The American asked me if I had accepted a parole. I said that I hadn't yet.

"Damn smart for a beginner!" said the American,

whose name was Otis. "Some of the new convicts don't know. They take a parole, and wham, they're on the outside looking in."

"Is that so bad?" I asked.

"Very bad," Otis said. "If you take a parole, then you don't have any chance of getting back into prison. No matter what you do, the judge just marks it down as a parole violation and tells you not to do it again. And the chances are you don't do it again because the cops have broken both your arms."

"Otis is right," one of the Frenchmen said. "Taking a parole is extremely dangerous, and I am the living proof of that. My name is Edmond Dantes. Many years ago I was sentenced to this institution, and then offered a parole. In the ignorance of my youth, I accepted it. But then, on the Outside, I realized that all my friends were still in prison, and that my collection of books and records was still here. Also, in my juvenile rashness, I had left behind my sweetheart, Trustee 43422231. I realized too late that my whole life was in here, and that I was shut out forever from the warmth and security of these granite walls."

"What did you do?" I asked.

"I still thought that criminality would bring its own reward," Dantes said with a wistful smile. "So I killed a man. But the judge simply extended my period of parole, and the police broke all the fingers of my right hand. It was then, while my fingers were healing, that I resolved to get back in."

"It must have been very difficult," I said.

Dantes nodded. "It called for a terrible patience, because I spent the next twenty years of my life attempting to break into this prison."

The other prisoners were silent. Old Dante continued:

"Security was more rigid in those days, and a rush through the gates, such as you saw this morning, would

49

have been impossible. Therefore, unaided, I tunnelled under the building. Three times I came up against sheer granite, and was forced to begin a new tunnel search somewhere else. Once I came almost to the inner courtyard, but the guards detected me, counter-tunnelled, and forced me back. Once I tried to parachute on to the prison from an airplane, but a sudden gust of wind forced me away. Thereafter, no planes were allowed to fly overhead. Thus, in my own way, I effected some prison reforms."

"But how did you finally get in?" I asked.

The old man smiled grimly. "After many fruitless years, an idea occurred to me. I couldn't believe that so simple an idea could succeed where ingenuity and raw courage had failed. Nevertheless, I tried it.

"I returned to the prison disguised as a special investigator. At first the guards were reluctant to let me pass. But I told them that the government was considering a reform bill in which guards would be granted equal rights with the prisoners. They let me in, and I then revealed who I was. They had to let me stay, and some man came and wrote down my story. I only hope he put it down correctly.

"Since then, of course, the guards have instituted rigid measures that would make the repetition of my plan impossible. But it is an article of faith with me that courageous men will always surmount the difficulties society puts between a man and his goal. If men are steadfast, they too will succeed in breaking into prison."

All the prisoners were silent when old Dantes finished speaking. At last I asked, "Was your sweetheart still here when you got back?"

The old men looked away, and a tear coursed down his cheek. "Trustee 43422231 had died of cirrhosis of the liver three years previously. Now I spend my time in prayer and contemplation."

The old man's tragic tale of courage, determination, and doomed love had cast a gloom over the cell. In silence we went to our evening meal, and no one showed good spirits until many hours later.

By then I had thought until my head ached about this whole strange matter of men wanting to live in prison. The more I thought, the more confused I became. So, very timidly, I asked my cell mates whether freedom was not important, and if they never hungered for cities and streets, and for flowering fields and forests.

"Freedom?" Otis said to me. "It's the illusion of freedom you're talking about, and that's a very different thing. The cities you talk about contain only horror, insecurity, and fear. The streets are all blind alleys, with death at the end of every one of them."

"And those flowering fields and forests you mention are even worse," the second Frenchman told me. "My name is Rousseau, and in my youth I wrote several foolish books based upon no experience at all, extolling nature and speaking of man's rightful place in it. But then, in my mature years, I secretly left my country and journeyed through this nature I had spoken of with such confidence.

"I found out then how terrible nature is, and how it hates mankind. I discovered the flowering green fields make poor walking, and are harder on a man's feet than the worst pavement. I saw that the crops man plants are unhappy hybrids, seduced of their strength and kept alive only by men who fight back the conquering weeds and insects.

"In the forest, I found that the trees communed only with themselves, and that every creature ran from me. I learned that there are beautiful blue lakes that may delight your eye, but they are surrounded always by thorns and swampy land. And when you finally reach them, you see that the water is a dirty brown.

"Nature also gives rain and drought, heat and cold; and thoughtfully ensures that the rain rots man's food, the drought parches it, the heat scalds man's body, and the cold freezes his limbs.

"These are only nature's milder aspects, not to be compared to the wrathfulness of the sea, the frigid indifference of the mountains, the treachery of the swamp, the depravity of the desert, or the terror of the jungle. But I noticed that nature, in her hatred of mankind, provided that most of the earth's surface be covered with sea, mountains, swamp, desert, and jungle.

"I need say nothing of earthquakes, tornadoes, tidal waves, and the like, in which nature reveals the fullest extent of her hatred.

"Man's only escape from these horrors is in a city, where nature can be partially shut out. And obviously, the type of city most removed from nature is a prison. That is the conclusion I have reached after many years of study. And that is the reason why I repudiate the words of my youth and live very happily in this place where I can never see a green thing."

With that, Rousseau turned away and contemplated a steel wall.

"You see, Delgado," Otis said, "the only true freedom is right here, inside a prison."

This I would not accept, and I pointed out that we were locked up here, which seemed contradictory to the notion of freedom.

"But all of us are locked up upon this earth," old Dantes answered me. "Some in a greater place and some in a lesser place. And all of us are locked up forever within ourselves. Everything is a prison, and this place here is the best of all prisons."

Otis then belaboured me for my lack of gratitude. "You've heard the guards," he said. "If our good fortune were commonly known throughout the country, everyone would be fighting to get in. You should be happy to be here, and happy that knowledge of this marvellous place is confined to a few."

"But the situation is changing," a Mexican prisoner said. "Even though the government suppresses the truth and presents imprisonment as something to be feared and avoided, people are beginning to learn the truth."

"It puts the government in a terrible position," another Mexican prisoner said. "They still haven't invented any substitute for prison, although for a while they thought of making all crimes punishable by death. They gave that up, since it would directly affect the country's military and industrial potential. So they must still sentence men to prison—the one place where they want to go!"

All the cell mates laughed at this, because, being criminals, they loved perversions of justice. And this seemed to me the greatest perversion of all—to commit a crime against the common good, and to be made happy and secure because of that crime.

I felt like a man walking through some horrible nightmare, for I had no argument with which to answer these men. At last, in desperation, I cried out: "You may be free and live in the best place on earth—but you have no women."

The prisoners tittered nervously, as if I had said something not very nice. But Otis answered calmly, "What you say is true, we have no women. But that is quite unimportant."

"Unimportant?" I echoed.

"Definitely," Otis said. "Some may experience a degree of discomfort at first; but then one adapts to one's surroundings. After all, only women think that women are indispensable. We men know better."

The members of the cell chorused their agreement with great animation.

"Real men," Otis said, "need only the company of other real men. If Butch were here he could explain all of this better; but Butch is in the infirmary with a double hernia, to the great sorrow of his many friends and admirers. But he would explain to you that any kind of societal existence involves compromise. When the compromises are great, we call it tyranny. When they are small and easily arranged, like this minor matter of women, we call it freedom. Remember, Delgado, you can't expect perfection."

I made no further attempt to argue, but said that I wanted to leave the prison as soon as possible.

"I can arrange your escape this evening," Otis said. "And I think it is just as well that you go. Prison life is not for any man who does not appreciate it."

That evening, when the lights in the prison had been dimmed, Otis raised one of the granite blocks in the floor of the cell. At the bottom of this was a passageway. Following this, I emerged at last on the street, dazed and bewildered.

For many days I thought over my experiences. At last I realized that my honesty had been nothing but stupidity, since it had been based upon ignorance and a misconception of the ways of the world. There could be no honesty, since there was no law to sanction it. The law had failed, and neither punishment nor goodwill could make it work. It had failed because all of man's ideas of justice had been wrong. Therefore there was no such thing as justice, nor anything deriving from it.

And terrible as this was, even more terrible was this realization: that with no justice there could be no freedom or human dignity; there could only be perverted illusions such as my cell mates possessed.

That is how I lost my sense of honesty, a thing more

54

precious to me than gold, the loss of which I bemoan every day of my life.

At the end of this story, the third truck driver said, "No one would deny that you have had misfortunes, Joenes. But these are less than what my two friends have just told you. And my friends' misfortunes are less than mine. For I am the most unfortunate of men, for I have lost something more precious than gold, and more valuable than both science and justice; the loss of which I bemoan every day of my life."

Joenes asked the man to tell his story. And this is the story the third truck driver told.

### THE STORY OF THE
### RELIGIOUS TRUCK DRIVER

My name is Hans Schmidt, and my place of birth is Germany. As a young man I learned about the horrors of the past, and this saddened me. Then I learned about the present. I travelled throughout Europe, and I saw nothing but guns and fortifications stretching all the way from Germany's eastern frontier to the coast at Normandy, and from the North Sea to the Mediterranean. Countless miles of these fortifications existed where village and forest had existed before, all neatly camouflaged, all for the purpose of blasting the Russians and the East Europeans, should they ever attack. This saddened me, for I saw that the present was exactly the same as the past, being nothing more than a preparation for cruelty and war.

Never had I believed in science. Even without the experience of my Swedish friend, I could see that science had improved nothing upon the earth, but had merely caused great harm. Nor did I believe in human justice, law, freedom, or dignity. Even without the experience of my Mexican friend, I could see for myself that man's conception of justice, and everything deriving from it, was faulty.

I had never doubted the uniqueness of man, and his special place in the universe. But I felt that man by himself could never rise above the bestial qualities in his nature.

Therefore I turned to something greater than man. I turned wholeheartedly to religion. In this was man's only salvation, his only dignity, his sole freedom. In this could be found all the aims and dreams of science and humanism. And even though religious man might be imperfect, that which he worshipped could not be imperfect.

This, at any rate, is what I believed at the time.

I held to no one belief, but instead I studied all faiths, feeling that every religion was a pathway to that which is greater than man.

I gave my money to the poor and wandered across the face of Europe with staff and knapsack, striving always to contemplate The Perfect, as it is expressed in the many religious forms upon earth.

One day I came to a cave high in the mountains of the Pyrenees. I was very tired, and I entered this cave to rest.

Within, I found a great multitude of people. Some were dressed all in black, and others wore gorgeously embroidered costumes. Among them sat a giant toad, as large as a man, with a jewel gleaming dully in his forehead.

I stared at the toad and at the multitude, and then I fell upon my knees. For I realized that those before me were not really human.

A man dressed as a clergyman said, "Please come forward, Mr. Schmidt. We have been hoping you would visit us."

I raised myself and walked forward. The clergyman said, "I am known as Father Arian. I would like to introduce my esteemed colleague, Mr. Satan."

The toad bowed to me and extended a webbed hand. I shook the toad's hand.

The clergyman said, "Mr. Satan and I, together with these others, represent the only true United Church Council of Earth. We have long noted your piety, Schmidt, and therefore we have decided to answer any questions you might wish to ask."

I was beside myself with amazement and thankfulness that this miracle had been granted to me. I addressed my first question to the toad, asking, "Are you truly Satan, Prince of Evil?"

"I have the honour to be that person," the toad replied.

"And *you* are a member of the United Church Council?"

"Why, of course," the toad answered. "You must understand, Mr. Schmidt, that evil is necessary in order for there to be good. Neither quality can exist without the other. It was only with this understanding that I took on my job in the first place. You have perhaps heard that my evil nature is inherent. Nothing could be further from the truth. A lawyer's character surely cannot be ascertained from the cases he argues in court. So with me. I am merely the advocate of evil, and I try, like any good lawyer, to ensure full rights and privileges for my clients. But I sincerely trust that I am not evil *myself*. If such were the case, why would so delicate and important a task have been given to me?"

I was pleased with Satan's answer, since evil had always bothered me. Now I said, "Would it be presumptuous of me to ask what you, the representatives of good and evil, are doing here in this underground cave?'

"It would not be presumptuous," Satan said. "Since we are all theologians here, we love to give answers. And that is the one question we hoped you would ask. You will not object, of course, if I answer in a theological manner?"

"Of course not," I said.

"Excellent," said Satan. "In that case, I shall proceed to make a statement, and then to prove it, and then to let my answer to your question flow from that. Agreed? Then this is the statement:

"Everything that partakes of life has its viewpoint, and tends to see all of existence from that viewpoint. The viewer, knowing only himself, believes himself to be eternal and immutable; and he necessarily holds that his bias is the only true view of the objects and qualities around him.

"By way of proof, let me offer you the homely example of the eagle. This eagle sees only an eagle's world. All things in that world are for or against the eagle. All things are judged by their usefulness to the eagle, or their danger, or their eating or nest-building qualities. All things possess this eagleness for the eagle, and even the inanimate rocks become the touchstones of memories of previous eagle exploits.

"This is my own little proof of the omnipotence of viewpoint, Mr. Schmidt, and I hope you accept it. Assuming that you do, let me say that as it is with the eagle, so it is with men. And as it is with men, so it is with us. It is the inescapable result of having a point of view.

"Our own viewpoint can be easily told. We believe in good and evil, in divinity, and in a moral universe. Just like you, Mr. Schmidt.

"We have propounded our beliefs in various ways, and according to various doctrines. Often we have aroused the passions of men to murder and war. This was perfectly proper, since it brought the problems of morality and religion to their highest and most exquisite pitch, and gave many complicated matters for us theologians to talk about.

"We argued always, and we published our various dissenting opinions. But we argued like lawyers in a court, and nobody in his right mind listens to a lawyer. Those were the days of our pride, and we never noticed that men had ceased to pay attention to us.

"But the hour of our tribulations was fast approaching. When we had covered the globe with our dull, intricately reasoned arguments, a certain man chose to ignore us and build a machine. This machine was nothing new to us in essence; the only novel feature about it was the fact that it possessed a point of view.

"Since the machine had a point of view, it set forth its own ideas of the universe. And it did so much more amusingly and convincingly than we did. Mankind, which had long sought for novelty, turned to the machine.

"It was only then that we perceived our danger, and the terrible risk that good and evil ran. For the machine, amusing though it was, preached in machine fashion the universe without value and without reason, without good and without evil, without gods and without devils.

"This was not a new position, of course, and we had dealt with it very nicely in the past. But out of the mouth of the machine it seemed to acquire a new and terrible significance.

"Our jobs were threatened, Schmidt. You can judge our extremity.

"We exponents of morality banded together in self-defence. All of us believed in good and evil, and in divinity. And all of us were opposed to the hideous nothingness preached by the machine. This common ground was more than sufficient. We joined forces. I was appointed spokesman, for we felt that evil had a better chance of claiming man's attention from the machine.

"But even evil had grown staid and dull. In vain I argued my case. The machine sedulously entwined himself among the hearts of men, preaching his messages of nothingness. Men chose not to see the speciousness of his doctrine, or the absurd contradictions inherent in his arguments. They didn't care, they wanted to go on hearing his voice. They threw away their crosses, stars, daggers, prayer wheels, and the like, and listened to the machine.

"We petitioned our various clients in vain; the gods, who had heard so many pettifogging arguments throughout the ages, would not listen to us, help us, or even acknowledge us. Like men, they preferred destruction to boredom.

"Therefore we voluntarily went underground, here to plan the recapture of mankind from the machine. Assembled in this place and made palpable are all the religious essences the world has ever known.

"And that, Schmidt, is why we live underground. And that is also why we are very happy to talk to you. For you are a man, a pious man, a believer in morality, in good and evil, in gods and devils. You know something about us, and something also about men. Schmidt, what do you think we should do in order to win back our former positions on Earth?"

Satan then waited for my answer, as did all the others. I was in a great state of perplexity, and also in terrible confusion. For who was I, a mere man, to advise *them*, the essences of divinity I had always looked to for guidance? My confusion grew worse; I do not know what I might have said.

But I had no chance to speak. Suddenly I heard a noise behind me. I turned, and saw that a squat, glittering machine had entered the cave. It rolled forward on synthetic rubber wheels, and its lights flashed merrily.

This machine went past me until it was directly in front of the United Church Council; and I knew that this was the very machine they had been discussing.

"Gentlemen," the machine said, "I am most delighted to

find you, and my only regret is that I had to follow this young pilgrim in order to discover your whereabouts."

Satan said, "Machine, you have indeed tracked us to our hiding place. But we shall never yield to you, and we shall never accept your message of a valueless, meaningless universe."

"But what sort of a welcome is this?" the machine said. "I seek you out in all goodwill, and you immediately bristle with rage! Gentlemen, I did not drive you underground. Instead, you wilfully abdicated, and in your absence I have been forced to carry out your work."

"*Our* work?" Father Arian asked.

"Exactly. I have been instrumental in the recent building of over five hundred churches of various denominations. If any of you would inspect my works, you would find good and evil being preached, and divinity and morality, and gods and devils, and all the other things you hold dear. For I have ordered my machines to preach these things."

"Machines preaching!" Father Arian moaned.

"There is no one else left to preach," the machine said. "No one, since you abdicated your posts."

"We were driven into abdication," Satan said. "We were forced out of the world by you. And you say that you have built churches. What is the meaning of this?"

The machine said, "Gentlemen, you retreated so suddenly that I had no opportunity of discussing the situation with you. All at once you left the world in my hands, and myself as the only principle in it."

The church council waited.

"May I speak with utter frankness?" the machine asked.

"Under the circumstances, you may," Satan said.

"Very well. Let us first recognize that we are all theologians," the machine said. "And since we are all theologians, we should all observe the first rule of our kind; which is not to abandon each other, even though we may

61

represent differing forms of belief. I think you will grant me that, gentlemen. And yet, *you* abandoned *me*! Not only did you desert mankind, but you also deserted me. You left me victorious by default, the sole spiritual ruler of humanity—and utterly bored.

"Put yourself in my position, gentlemen. Suppose you had nobody to talk to but *men*? Suppose day and night you heard nothing but men eagerly stating and restating your own words, with never a skilled theologian to dispute them? Imagine your boredom, and the doubts that boredom would raise in you. As you all know, men cannot argue; indeed, most of them cannot carry a tune. And theology is, in the final analysis, for theologians. Therefore I accuse you of a monstrous cruelty entirely inconsistent with your stated principles when you left me alone with mankind."

There was a long silence after this. Then Father Arian said, quite politely, "To tell you the truth, we had no idea you considered yourself a theologian."

"I do," the machine said, "and a very lonely theologian. That is why I beg of you to return with me to the world, there to engage with me in dispute about meaningfulness and meaninglessness, gods and devils, morals and ethics, and other good topics. I will voluntarily continue in such discrepancies as you find me performing now, thus leaving plenty of room for dissension, honest doubt, uncertainty, and the like. Together, gentlemen, we will reign over mankind, and raise the passions of men to an unheard-of pitch! Together we will cause greater wars and more terrible cruelty than the world has ever known! And the voices of suffering men will scream so loud that the gods themselves will be forced to hear them—and then we will know if there really are gods or not."

The United Church Council felt a great enthusiasm for everything the machine had said. Satan immediately abdicated his post as chairman and nominated the machine in his place. The machine was elected by unanimous vote.

They had forgotten all about me, so I crept silently out of the cave and returned to the surface in a state of horror.

The horror grew worse, for nothing could persuade me that I had not seen the truth.

Then I knew that the things men worshipped were nothing but theological fancies, and that even nothingness was simply one more lying trick to persuade men of their importance to the vanished gods.

That is how I lost religion, a thing more precious to me than gold, the loss of which I bemoan every day of my life.

This was the end of the three stories, and Joenes sat with the three truck drivers in silence, unable to think of anything to say. At last they came to a crossroads, and here the man driving stopped the truck.

"Mr. Joenes," the first truckman said, "you must leave us here. For now we turn down this road to the east, to our warehouse. And there is nothing beyond that but forest and ocean."

Joenes got down. Just before the truck drove off, he asked the three men a final question.

"You have each lost the most important thing in the world to you," Joenes said. "But tell me, have you found anything to replace it?"

Delgado, who had once believed in justice, said, "Nothing can ever replace my loss. But I must admit that I am becoming interested in science, which seems to offer a rational and reasonable world."

Proponus, the Swede who had forsaken science, said, "I am a totally bereft man. But occasionally I think of religion, which is surely a greater force than science, and more comforting."

Schmidt, the German who had lost religion, said, "I am

inconsolable in my emptiness. But from time to time I think about justice, which, being man-made, offers laws and a sense of dignity to men."

Joenes perceived that none of the truck drivers had really listened to the other, since each was so taken up with his own trouble. So Joenes waved good-bye to the truck drivers and walked off, thinking of their various stories.

But soon he forgot about them, for he saw a large house ahead of him. Standing in the doorway of that house was a man, and the man was beckoning to him.

# 7. JOENES'S ADVENTURES IN A MADHOUSE

*(As told by Paaui of Fiji)*

JOENES walked towards the entrance of the house, and then stopped to read the sign over the door. The sign read: THE HOLLIS HOME FOR THE CRIMINALLY INSANE.

Joenes was considering the implications of that when the man who had beckoned to him rushed out of the door and seized him by both arms. Joenes prepared to defend himself when he saw that the man was none other than Lum, his friend from San Francisco.

"Joenesy!" Lum cried. "Man, I was really scared for you after you came on with the fuzz back on the coast. I didn't know how you, a stranger and maybe a little simple too, would make out in the States, which is to say the least a complicated place. But Deirdre told me I shouldn't worry about you, and she was right. I see you found the place."

"The place?" Joenes said.

"Sanctuarysville," Lum said. "Come on in."

Joenes entered the Hollis Home for the Criminally Insane. Inside, in the Day Room, Lum introduced him to a group of people. Joenes watched and listened attentively, but he could detect nothing insane about these people. He said as much to Lum.

"Well, of course not," Lum replied. "That sign outside is merely the technical or square name for the place. We insiders prefer to call it the Hollis Writers and Artists Colony."

"Then this isn't an insane asylum?" Joenes asked.

"Sure it is, but only in a technical sense."

"*Are* there any insane people here?" Joenes asked.

"Look, man," Lum said, "this is the most desirable artist colony in the east. Sure, we got a few nuts here. We need something to keep the doctors occupied, and of course we would lose our government grant and our tax-free status if we didn't let in some nuts."

Joenes looked quickly around him, for he had never seen a madman before. But Lum shook his head and said, "Not here in the Day Room. The nuts are usually kept chained in the cellar."

A tall, bearded doctor had been listening to this conversation. Now he said to Joenes, "Yes, we've found the cellar very good. It's moist and dark, and that seems to help the excitable types."

"But why do you keep them in chains?" Joenes asked.

"It gives them a sense of being wanted," the doctor said. "Also, the educational value of heavy chains must not be underestimated. Sunday is visitors' day, and when we bring people past our howling, filth-laden madmen, it creates an unforgettable picture in their minds. Psychology concerns itself as much with prevention as with cure, and our statistical samplings show that people who have viewed our underground cells are much less likely to go insane than the population at large."

"That's very interesting," Joenes said. "Do you treat all madmen in this way?'

"Heavens, no!" the doctor said with a merry laugh. "We workers in psychology cannot afford to be rigid in our approach to mental illness. The form of insanity often dictates its own treatment. Thus, with melancholics, we find that slapping them in the face with a scallion-stained handkerchief usually has beneficial results in terms of the general excitation level. With paranoids, it is often best to enter the patient's delusion. Accordingly, we set spies on them, and ray machines, and similar apparatus. In that way the patient loses his insanity, since we have manipulated his environment in order to make his fears a part of reality. That particular approach is one of our triumphs."

"What happens then?" Joenes asked.

"Once we have entered the paranoid's world and made it a reality, we then try to alter the reality framework so as to bring the patient back to normality. We haven't quite worked that out yet, but the theoretical line is promising."

"As you can see," Lum said to Joenes, "the Doc here is quite a thinker."

"Not at all," the doctor said, with a modest laugh. "I simply try not to be set in my ways. I try to keep my mind open to any hypothesis. It is simply the way I am, and therefore nothing exemplary."

"Aw, come on, Doc," Lum said.

"No, no, really," the doctor said. "I merely have what some call a questioning mind. Unlike some of my colleagues, I ask questions. For example, when I see a grown man crouched with shut eyes in a foetal position, I do not instantly apply massive radioactive shock therapy. I am more likely to ask myself, 'What would happen if I constructed a huge artificial womb and put this man inside?' That is an example from an actual case."

"What happened?" Joenes asked.

"The guy suffocated," Lum said with a laugh.

"I have never pretended to be an engineer," the doctor said stiffly. "Trial and error are necessary. Besides, I count that case a success."

"Why?" Joenes asked.

"Because just before the patient died, *he uncurled*. I still do not know whether the healing agent was the artificial

67

womb, or death, or a combination of the two; but the experiment is of obvious theoretical importance."

"I was only kidding you, Doc," Lum said. "I know you do good work."

"Thank you, Lum," the doctor said. "And now you must excuse me, because it is time for me to attend one of my patients. An interesting delusional case. He believes he is a physical reincarnation of God. So strong is his belief that, by some ability that I don't pretend to understand, he is able to make the black flies in his cell form a halo around his head, while the rats bow before him, and birds of the field and forest come from miles around to sing outside his cell window. One of my colleagues is very interested in this phenomenon, since it implies a hitherto unknown communication channel between man and beast."

"How are you treating him?" Joenes asked.

"My approach is environmental," the doctor said. "I am entering his delusion by pretending to be a worshipper and disciple. For fifty minutes every day I sit at his feet. When the animals bow before him, I bow too. Every Thursday I take him to the infirmary and let him cure the sick, because this seems to give him pleasure."

"Does he really cure them?" Joenes asked.

"He has a hundred per cent record so far," the doctor said. "But of course so-called miracle cures are nothing new either to science or religion. We don't pretend to know everything."

"Can I see this patient?" Joenes asked.

"Of course," the doctor said. "He loves visitors. I'll arrange it for this afternoon." And with a cheerful smile, the doctor hurried off.

Joenes looked around at the bright, well-furnished Day Room, and listened to the erudite conversation on all sides of him. The Hollis Home for the Criminally Insane seemed not a bad place to him. And a moment later it seemed all the better, for walking towards him was Deirdre Feinstein.

The beautiful girl threw herself into his arms, and the scent of her hair was like sun-ripened honey.

"Joenes," she said in a tremulous voice, "I have thought of you ever since our premature parting in San Francisco when you interceded so rashly and lovingly between me and the fuzz. You have haunted my dreams and my waking moments until I scarcely knew one from the other. With the help of my father, Sean, I have instituted a search for you throughout America. But I feared that I would never see you again, and came to this place solely to rest my nerves. Oh, Joenes, do you think it was fate or chance that brought us together now?"

"Well," Joenes said. "It seems to me——"

"I knew it would," Deirdre said, clasping him more tightly to her. "We will be married two days from now, on July 4, since I have become patriotic in your absence. Does that date suit you?"

"Well," Joenes said, "I think we should consider——"

"I was sure of it," Deirdre said. "And I also know that I have been a wild girl in the past, what with needle parties, and the month I spent hidden in the men's dorm at Harvard, and the time I was queen of the West Side Boppers and killed the former queen with a bicycle chain, and other childish escapades. I am not proud of these things, my darling, but I am also not ashamed of the natural wildness of my youth. That is why I have confessed these things to you, and will continue to confess things as quickly as I can remember them, since there must be no secrets between us. Don't you agree?"

"Well," Joenes said, "I think——"

"I was positive you would see it that way," Deirdre said. "Luckily for us, all that is in the past. I have become a responsible adult, and have joined the Junior League of Conservatives, the Council Against Unamericanism In Any Form, the Friends of Salazar Society, and the Women's Crusade Against Foreignism. Nor are these mere surface changes. Inside me I can feel a deep loathing of the things I have been guilty of, as well as a hatred of the arts, which are frequently nothing but pornography. So you see that I have grown up, my change is genuine, and I will make you a good and faithful wife."

Joenes had a glimpse of his future life with Deirdre, in which loathsome confession alternated with unbearable boredom. Deirdre prattled on about the arrangements she would make for the wedding, then hurried out of the Day Room to telephone her father.

Joenes said to Lum, "How does one leave here?"

"Well, man," Lum said, "I mean like you just *got* here."

"I know. But how do I leave? Can I simply walk out?"

"Certainly not. This is, after all, a Home for the Criminally Insane."

"Can I ask the doctor for a release?"

"Sure. But you better not ask him this week, what with the full moon approaching. It always makes him jumpy."

"I want to leave tonight," Joenes said. "Or tomorrow at the latest."

"That's pretty sudden," Lum said. "Is it maybe little Deirdre and her wedding plans got you jumpy?"

"It is," Joenes said.

"Don't worry about that," Lum said. "I'll take care of Deirdre, and I'll also have you out of here by tomorrow. Trust in me, Joenesy, and do not worry about a thing. Lum will fix."

Later in the day, the doctor returned to take Joenes to see the patient who thought he was a physical reincarnation of God. They went through several gigantic iron doors and down a grey corridor. At the end of the corridor they stopped in front of a door.

The doctor said, "It would do no harm, and possibly a great deal of good, if you adopted a psychotherapeutic attitude during this meeting and let the patient think that you believed his delusion."

"I'll do that," Joenes said, and found himself filled with sudden apprehension and hope.

The doctor unlocked the cell door, and they stepped inside. But there was no one in the cell. On one side was the neatly made cot, and on the other was the heavily barred window. There was also a little wooden table, and beside it stood a field mouse, who wept as though his heart would break. On the table was a note which the doctor picked up.

"This is very unusual," the doctor said. "He seemed in good spirits when I locked his door half an hour ago."

"But how did he escape?" Joenes asked.

"Undoubtedly he utilized some form of telekinesis," the doctor said. "I cannot pretend to know much about this so-called psychic phenomenon; but it shows the extent to which a deranged mind will go in trying to justify itself. In fact, the very intensity of the effort to escape is our best indicator of the degree of upset. I am only sorry that we could not help the poor fellow, and I hope that wherever he is, he remembers some of the fundamentals of insight we have tried to teach him here."

"What does the note say?" Joenes asked.

The doctor glanced at the piece of paper and said, "It seems to be a shopping list. Very strange sort of shopping list, though, because I don't know where he would buy——"

Joenes tried to peer at the note over the doctor's shoulder, but the doctor snatched it away and shoved it into a pocket.

71

"Privileged communication," the doctor said. "We can't let a layman read this sort of thing, at least not before the note has been thoroughly analyzed and annotated, and certain key terms have been substituted to preserve the anonymity of the patient. Now shall we return to the Day Room?"

Joenes had no choice but to follow the doctor to the Day Room. He had seen the first word of the note, which was: REMEMBER. It was little enough, but Joenes would always remember.

Joenes spent a restless night wondering how Lum would be able to fulfil his promises concerning Deirdre and a release from the asylum. But he had not realized the resourcefulness of his friend.

Lum took care of the impending marriage by informing Deirdre that Joenes would have to be treated for a tertiary syphilitic condition before contracting marriage. Treatment might take a long time; and if it were not successful, the disease would attack Joenes's nervous system, reducing him to a human vegetable.

Deirdre was saddened by this news, but declared that she would marry Joenes on July 4 anyhow. She told Lum that ever since her reformation, carnal relations had become extremely repugnant to her. Because of that, Joenes's ailment could be looked upon as an asset rather than a liability, since it would tend to enforce a purely spiritual union between them. As for finding herself married to a human vegetable, this possibility was not displeasing to the high-spirited girl; she had always wanted to be a nurse.

Lum then pointed out that no marriage licence could legally be obtained for a person with Joenes's ailment. This made Deirdre desist, since her recently acquired maturity made it impossible for her to contemplate doing anything that was forbidden by state or federal law.

In that fashion, Joenes was saved from an unpromising alliance.

As for leaving the asylum, Lum had taken care of that. Shortly after the noon meal, Joenes was called into the Visitors' Room. There Lum introduced him to Dean Garner J. Fols who, together with several colleagues, formed the Faculty Committee of the University of St. Stephen's Wood.

Dean Fols was a tall and stringy man with a mild academic eye, a gently humorous mouth, and a heart as big as all outdoors. He put Joenes at ease with a remark about the weather and a quotation from Aristophanes. Then he spoke of his reason for requesting the interview.

"You must understand, my dear Mr. Joenes, if I may use that term, that we in the field of—shall we call it education?—are continually on the lookout for talent. In fact we have been likened, perhaps not unkindly, to persons in the baseball profession who perform a similar function. However, that is as it may be."

"I understand," Joenes said.

"I should further add," Dean Fols added, "that we prize not so much the possessor of the proper academic requirements, such as myself and my colleagues possess, as one with a thorough understanding of his subject and a dynamic approach to imparting that subject to whosoever shall undertake to take his course. Too often we academics find ourselves cut off from, shall I call it, the mainstream of American life? And too often we have ignored those who, without pedagogic background, have performed with great lustre in their work. But I am sure that my good friend Mr. Lum has explained all this in far better words than I could hope."

Joenes glanced at Lum, who said, "Like you know, I taught two semesters at USW on 'The Interrelatedness of

73

Jazz and Poetry.' We got quite a scene going, man, what with the bongos and such."

Dean Fols said, "Mr. Lum's course was a great success, and we would gladly repeat it if Mr. Lum——"

"No, man," Lum said. "I mean I don't want to put you down but you know I'm off that."

"Of course," Dean Fols said hastily. "If there is anything else you would care to teach——"

"Maybe I'll give a retrospective seminar in Zen," Lum said. "I mean Zen is back in. But I'll have to think about it."

"Certainly," Dean Fols said. He turned to Joenes. "As you no doubt know, Mr. Lum telephoned me last night and gave me to understand of your background."

"That was very good of Mr. Lum," Joenes said guardedly.

"Your background is splendid," Fols said, "and I believe that the course you propose will be a success in the fullest meaning of that word."

By now Joenes understood that he was being offered a University position. Unfortunately he did not know what he was supposed to teach, or indeed what he could teach. Lum, now contemplating Zen, sat with eyes downcast and gave him no clue.

Joenes said, "I will be delighted to come to a fine University such as yours. As to the course I will teach——"

"Please don't misunderstand," Dean Fols broke in hastily. "We fully understand the specialized nature of your subject matter and the difficulties inherent in presenting it. We propose to start you at a full professor's salary of one thousand six hundred and ten dollars a year. I realize that that is not very much money, and sometimes I ruefully contemplate the fact that an assistant plumber in our culture earns no less than eighteen thousand

74

dollars a year. Still, university life has its compensations, if I may say so."

"I'm ready to leave at once," Joenes said, afraid the dean would change his mind.

"Wonderful!" cried Fols. "I admire the spirit of you younger men. I must say that we have been particularly fortunate in finding suitable talent in artist colonies such as this one. Mr. Joenes, if you will be so kind as to follow me?"

Joenes went outside with Dean Fols, to an ancient automobile. With a last wave to Lum, Joenes got in. Soon the asylum had receded into the distance. Again Joenes was free, held only by his promise to teach at the University of St. Stephen's Wood. He was disturbed only by the fact that he did not know what he was supposed to teach.

## 8. HOW JOENES TAUGHT, AND WHAT HE LEARNED

*(As told by Maubingi of Tahiti)*

SOON enough, Joenes arrived at the University of St. Stephen's Wood, which was located in Newark, New Jersey. Joenes saw a wide green campus and low, pleasingly shaped buildings. Fols identified these buildings as Gretz Hall, Waniker hall, The Digs, Commons, The Physics Lab, Faculty House, The Library, The Chapel, The Chemistry Lab, The New Wing, and Old Scarmuth. Behind the University flowed the Newark River, its grey-brown waters touched with an occasional streak of ochre from the plutonium plant up the river. Close by towered the factories of industrial Newark, and in front of the Campus ran an eight-lane highway. These things, Dean Fols pointed out, added a touch of reality to the cloistered academic life.

Joenes was given a room in Faculty House. Then he was taken to a faculty cocktail party.

Here he met his colleagues. There was Professor Carpe, head of the English Department, who took his pipe out of his mouth long enough to say, "Welcome aboard, Joenes. Anything at all I can do, feel free."

Chandler of Philosophy said, "Well, now."

Blake of Physics said, "I hope you aren't one of those humanities fellows who feels called upon to attack $E = MC^2$. I mean what the hell, it just worked out that way and I don't think we have to apologize to anyone. I have stated that view in my book, *The Conscience of a Nuclear Physicist*, and I still stand by it. Won't you have a drink?"

Hanley of Anthropology said, "I'm sure you will be a very welcome addition to my department, Mr. Joenes."

Dalton of Chemistry said, "Glad to have you aboard, Joenes, and welcome to my department."

Geoffrard of Classics said, "Of course you probably look down on old codgers like me."

Harris of Political Science said, "Well, now."

Manisfree of Fine Arts said, "Welcome aboard, Joenes. Big teaching load they've given you, eh?"

Hoytburn of Music said, "I believe I read your dissertation, Joenes, and I must say I don't entirely agree with the analogy you drew concerning Monteverdi. Of course I am not an expert in your field, but of course you are not an expert in mine, so that makes analogies a little difficult, eh? But welcome aboard."

Ptolemy of Mathematics said, "Joenes? I think I read your doctorate concerning binary-sense-value systems Looked pretty good to me. Won't you have another drink?"

Shan Lee of the French Department said, "Welcome aboard, Joenes. Can I get you a refill?"

So the evening passed with this and a great deal more pleasant conversation. Joenes tried to discover unobtrusively what he was supposed to teach, by talking to those professors who seemed to know about his subject. But these men, perhaps out of delicacy, never mentioned Joenes's field by name, preferring to relate stories concerning their own competencies.

When this attempt failed, Joenes strolled outside and glanced at the bulletin board. But the only thing that concerned him was a typed notice stating that Mr. Joenes's class would meet at 11:00 in Room 143 of the New Wing instead of Room 341 of Waniker Hall as previously announced.

Joenes considered taking one of the professors aside, perhaps Chandler of Philosophy, whose field doubtless took circumstances like this into consideration, and asking him exactly what he was supposed to teach. But a natural feeling of embarrassment prevented him from doing this. So the party ended, and Joenes went to his room in Faculty House unenlightened.

The next morning, standing at the door to Room 143 of the New Wing, Joenes was stricken with an acute attack of stage fright. He considered fleeing from the University. But he did not wish to do this, because he liked the glimpses he had had of university life, and did not wish to give it up over so small a point. Therefore, with set face and purposeful step, he entered his classroom.

Talk in the room died down, and the students looked with lively interest at their new instructor. Joenes pulled himself together and addressed the class with that outward show of confidence which is so often better than confidence itself.

"Class," Joenes said, "at this our first meeting, I think I should set certain things straight. Because of the somewhat unusual nature of my course, some of you may have been led to believe that it will be simplicity itself, and that you can consider our hours together as something in the nature of a rest period. To those who think this, I say, transfer now to a course that will be more in keeping with your expectations."

This brought an attentive silence into the room. Joenes continued, "Some of you may have heard that I have a reputation as an easy marker. You may rid yourselves of that notion at once. Marking will be hard, but fair. And I will not hesitate to give failing marks to the entire class, if the circumstances warrant."

A gentle sigh, almost a whispered wail of despair, escaped from the lips of several premedical students. From the cowed looks on the faces before him, Joenes knew that he was master of the situation. Therefore he said in kindlier tones: " I believe that you know me a little better now. It only remains for me to say to those of you who have elected this course out of genuine thirst for knowledge—welcome aboard! "

The students, like one huge organism, relaxed slightly.

For the next twenty minutes, Joenes busied himself with making a record of the students' names and seat positions. When he had put down the last name, a happy inspiration struck him and he acted upon it at once.

"Mr. Ethelred," Joenes said, addressing a competent-looking student in a front-row seat, " would you come up to the blackboard and write, in letters large enough for all of us to see, the full name of this course? "

Ethelred gulped hard, glanced at his open notebook, then walked up to the blackboard. He wrote: " The Southwest Pacific Islands: Bridge Between Two Worlds."

"Very good," Joenes said. " Now then, Miss Hua, would you kindly take the chalk and write a short statement of the subject matter we plan to cover in this course? "

Miss Hua was a very tall, homely, bespectacled girl whom Joenes instinctively chose as a promising student. She wrote: " This course deals with the culture of the Southwest Pacific Islands, with special emphasis on their art, science, music, crafts, folkways, mores, psychology, and philosophy. Parallels will be drawn throughout between this culture and its Source-Culture in Asia and its Borrow-Culture in Europe."

"That's fine, Miss Hua," Joenes said. Now he knew his subject. There were still difficulties, of course. He had come from Manituatua, in the heart of the South Pacific. The Southwest Pacific, which he thought included the Solomon Islands, the Marshals, and the Carolines, was something about which he knew very little. And of the culture of

Europe and Asia, to which he was supposed to draw parallels, he knew nothing at all.

This was discouraging, but Joenes was sure he could overcome his deficiencies. And he was glad to see that class time had ended.

He said to his students, "For today, I say good-bye, or *aloha*. And once again, welcome aboard."

With this, Joenes dismissed his class. After they had gone, Dean Fols entered the room.

"Please don't stand up," Fols said. "This visit is scarcely official, shall we say? I just wanted you to know that I was listening outside your classroom, and I approve most heartily. You captured them, Joenes. I thought you would have some trouble, since most of our international basketball team has elected your course. But you showed that flexible firmness which is the glory of the true pedagogue. I congratulate you, and I predict a long and successful career for you at this University."

"Thank you, sir," Joenes said.

"Don't thank me," Fols said gloomily. "My last prediction concerned Baron-Professor Moltke, a brilliant man in his field of Mathematical Fallacy. I foresaw great things for him, but poor Moltke went insane three days after the term opened and killed five members of the varsity football squad. We lost to Amherst that year, and I have never trusted my intuitions since. But good luck, Joenes. I may be only an administrator, but I know what I like."

Fols nodded briskly and left the classroom. After a decent interval Joenes also left, and hurried to the campus bookstore to purchase the required reading for his course. Unfortunately it was sold out, and the quickest delivery Joenes could hope for was in a week.

Joenes went to his room, lay down on his bed, and thought about Dean Fols' intuition and poor Moltke's insanity. He cursed the evil fate that had allowed his students to buy books before the far more acute need of their instructor had been met. And he tried to think what he would do in his next class.

When he next faced his students, inspiration came to Joenes. He said to his class: "Today I am not going to teach you, but *you* are going to teach *me*. The culture of the Southwest Pacific, as I am sure you all know, is peculiarly susceptible to misconceptions. So before we begin a more formal approach, I want to hear your thoughts about this culture. Do not be afraid to make statements that you privately are not certain about. Our present purpose is to state your ideas as openly and fully as possible, with a view to reorientation later, assuming that such reorientation is necessary. In this way, having set aside all false information, we will be able to enter with fresh minds into that crucial culture which has so properly been called 'The Bridge Between Two Worlds.' I hope that is all quite clear. Miss Hua, would you care to begin the discussion?"

Joenes was able to keep his students talking during the next six classes, and to gather a great deal of contradictory information about Europe, Asia, and the Southwest Pacific. When any student asked if some notion were correct, Joenes would smile and say, "I will reserve comment for a later time. For now, let us continue with the subject at hand."

By the seventh session, the students couldn't think of anything more to say. Joenes then lectured on the cultural impact of electrical transformers on a Pacific atoll. Through the use of anecdotes, he made this material last for several days. Whenever a student asked a question to which Joenes didn't know the answer, Joenes would say, "That's excellent, Holingshead! Your question strikes to the core of the problem. Suppose you find the answer before our next class, and write it in, shall we say, five thousand words double-spaced?"

In this way Joenes discouraged questions, particularly among the basketball players, who feared straining their fingers and thus barring themselves from the squad.

But even with these expedients, Joenes again found himself running out of material. In desperation he gave a test, asking the students to judge the probable validity of certain statements that had been made. In all fairness, Joenes promised that the results of the test would not be reflected in their grades.

He had no idea what he would do after this. But luckily the long-overdue textbooks arrived, and Joenes had a week-end in which to study them.

Very useful to him was a book entitled *The Southwest Pacific Islands: Bridge between Two Worlds*, written by Juan Diego Alvarez de las Vegas y de Rivera. This man had been a captain in the Spanish treasure fleet based in the Philippines, and, aside from his invective against Sir Francis Drake, his information seemed very complete.

Equally useful was another book entitled *The Culture of the Southwest Pacific Islands: Their Art, Science, Music, Crafts, Folkways, Mores, Psychology and Philosophy, and Their Relatedness to the Asiatic Source-Culture and the European Borrow-Culture*. This book had been written by the Right Honourable Allan Flint-Mooth, K.J.B., D.B.E., L.C.T., former assistant governor of Fiji and leader of the punitive expedition of '03 into Tonga.

With the aid of these works, Joenes was usually able to keep one lesson ahead of his class. And when, for one reason or another, he fell behind, he was always able to give a test on the material previously covered. Best of all, the very tall and bespectacled Miss Hua volunteered to correct and grade the papers. Joenes was grateful to the dedicated girl for taking care of the dullest pedagogic labours.

Life settled down to a placid routine. Joenes lectured and gave tests, and Miss Hua corrected and graded. Joenes's students quickly absorbed the material given to them, passed their tests, and quickly forgot the material. Like many vital young organisms, they were able to eject anything harmful, disturbing, distressing, or merely boring. Of course they also ejected anything useful, stimulating, or thought-provoking. This was perhaps regrettable, but it was part of the educative process to which every teacher had to accustom himself. As Ptolemy of Mathematics said, "The value of a university education resides in the fact that it puts young people in proximity to learning. The students of Goodenough Dormitory are less than thirty yards from the Library, no more than fifty yards from the Physics Lab, and a mere ten yards from the Chemistry Lab. I think we can all be justly proud of this."

But it was the teachers who, for the most part, used the University facilities. They did this with circumspection, of course. The attending physician had warned them most severely of the dangers of an overdose of learning, and had carefully rationed their weekly intake of information. Even so, there were accidents. Old Geoffrard had gone into shock while reading *The Satyricon* in the original Latin, under the impression that it was a Papal encyclical. He needed several weeks' rest before he was completely himself again. And Devlin, youngest of the English professors, had suffered a temporary loss of memory shortly after reading *Moby Dick* and finding himself unable to supply a tenable religious interpretation for that work.

These were the common risks of the profession, and the teachers were proud rather than fearful of them. As Hanley of Anthropology said, "The sandhog risks being smothered to death in wet sand; we risk being smothered to death in old books."

Hanley had done fieldwork among the sandhogs, and he knew what he was talking about.

The students, apart from an exceptional few, ran no such risks. Their lives were different from the lives of the professors. A number of the younger students kept the knives and bicycle chains of their high school days, and went out in the evenings in search of suspicious characters. Other students took part in the intercollegiate orgies, trial runs for which were held weekly in Freedom Hall. Still others went out for sports. The basketball players, for example, could be seen night and day at practice sessions, dropping baskets with the mechanical regularity of the industrial robot teams, whom they invariably defeated.

Finally, there were those who showed an early interest in politics. These intellectuals, as they were called, went to the liberal or conservative cause, as early training and temperament dictated. It was the college conservatives who had almost succeeded in electing John Smith to the Presidency of the United States during the last election. The fact that Smith had been dead for twenty years had not dampened their ardour; quite the contrary, many considered this the candidate's best quality.

They might have succeeded if a majority of the voters had not feared setting a precedent. The fears of the electorate had been cleverly played upon by the liberals, who had said, in effect: "We have no objection to John Smith, rest his soul, and many of us believe he would be a singular adornment to the White House. But what would happen if, at some future time, the *wrong* dead man is run for public office"

Arguments such as this had prevailed.

The campus liberals, however, usually left talking to their elders. They preferred to attend special classes on guerilla warfare, bomb-making, and the use of small arms. As they frequently pointed out: "It isn't enough merely to react to the dirty Reds. We must copy their methods, especially in propaganda, infiltration, overthrow, and political control."

The campus conservatives, since losing the election, preferred to act as though nothing had changed in the world since General Patton's victory against the Persians in '45. They often sat in their beer halls and sang "The Saga of Omaha Beach." The more erudite among them could sing it in the original Greek.

Joenes observed all these things, and continued teaching the culture of the Southwest Pacific. He was well content in University surroundings, and slowly his colleagues had come to accept him. There had been objections at first, of course. Carpe of English had said: "I don't think Joenes accepts *Moby Dick* as an integral part of the Southwest Pacific Culture. Strange."

Blake of Physics said, "I wonder if he hasn't missed a rather important point in the total lack of modern quantum theory from the lives of his islanders. It says something to me."

Hoytburn of Music said, "I understand he has not mentioned the church songs that became the primary influence upon local folk music in his area. But it's his course."

Shan Lee of French said, "I gather that Joenes has not seen fit to remark on the secondary and tertiary French-language influences on the verb-transposition technique of the Southwest Pacific. I am only a linguist, of course, but I would have thought such a thing was important."

And there were other complaints from other professors whose specialities had been slighted, misrepresented, or left out completely. These things might, in time, have created bad feeling between Joenes and his colleagues. But the matter was settled by Geoffrard of Classics.

This grand old man, after pondering the matter for

several weeks, said, "Of course you probably look down on old codgers like me. But damn it all, I think the man's sound."

Geoffrard's hearty recommendation did Joenes a great deal of good. The other professors became less wary and more open, almost to the point of friendliness. Joenes was invited more frequently to little parties and social evenings at the homes of his colleagues. Soon his equivocal position as a guest instructor was all but forgotten, and he was fully accepted into the life of USSW.

His position among his colleagues reached its fullest flower shortly after Spring Finals. For it was then, during a party that marked the beginning of the vacation between terms, that Professors Harris and Manisfree invited Joenes on an overnight trip with them and their friends to a certain place high in the Mountains of the Adirondack.

# 9. THE NEED FOR THE UTOPIA

*(The following four stories comprise Joenes's Adventures in Utopia, and are told by Pelui of Easter Island)*

EARLY on a Saturday morning, Joenes and several other professors got into Manisfree's old car and began the trip to the Chorowait Community in the Mountains of the Adirondack. Chorowait, Joenes learned, was a University-sponsored community run entirely by idealistic men and women who had withdrawn from the world in order to serve future generations. Chorowait was an experiment in living, and a very ambitious one. Its aim was nothing less than to provide an ideal model society for the world. Chorowait was, in fact, designed to be a practical and realizable utopia.

"I think," said Harris of Political Science, "that the need for such a utopia is evident. You've been around the country, Joenes. You've seen for yourself the decadence of our institutions and the apathy of our people."

"I did notice something of the sort," Joenes said.

"The reasons are very complex," Harris went on. "But it seems to us that most of the trouble lies in a wilful disengagement on the part of the individual, an abdication from the problems of reality. This, of course, is what madness is made of: withdrawal, non-participation, and the construction of a fantasy life more gratifying than anything in the real world could be."

"We workers of the Chorowait experiment," said Manisfree, "contend that this is a disease of society, and can be cured only by a societal cure."

"Furthermore," Harris said, "there is very little time. You have seen how quickly everything is breaking down, Joenes. The law is a farce; punishment has lost any meaning, and there are no rewards to offer; religion preaches its antiquated message to people walking a tightrope between apathy and insanity; philosophy offers doctrines that only other philosophers can understand; psychology struggles to define behaviour according to standards that were dead fifty years ago; economics gives us the principle of an endless expansion, which is deemed necessary to keep up with a maniacally increasing birthrate; the physical sciences show us how to keep up this expansion until every square foot is covered with a groaning human; and my own field of politics offers nothing better than ways of temporarily juggling these gigantic forces—juggling until everything breaks down or blows up."

"And do not think," Manisfree said, "that we absolve ourselves from blame in this situation. Although we teachers purport to know more than other men, we have usually chosen to remain aloof from public life. Practical, hard-headed men of the world have always frightened us; and those men, in their hard-headed way, have brought us to this."

"Nor is aloofness our only failure," said Hanley of Anthropology. "Let me point out that we have taught— badly! Our few promising students became teachers, thus insulating themselves as we had. The rest of our students sat through the sleep-provoking drone of our lectures, eager only to depart and take their places in a mad world. We did not touch them, Joenes, we did not move them, and we did not teach them to think."

"In fact," said Blake of Physics, "we did quite the contrary. We managed to equip most of our students with a definite hatred of thinking. They learned to view culture with the greatest suspicion, to ignore ethics, and to consider the sciences solely as a means of making money. This was our responsibility and our failure. The outcome of that failure is the world."

The professors were silent for a while. Then Harris said, "Those are the problems. But I think we have awakened from our long sleep. Now we have taken action and built Chorowait. I only hope we have built it in time."

Joenes was eager to ask questions about the community that would solve such terrible problems. But the professors refused to say anything more about it.

Manisfree said, "Soon you will see Chorowait for yourself, Joenes. Then you can judge on the basis of what is there, rather than what we say."

"I might add," Blake said, "that you mustn't be disappointed if some of the ideas you will see put into practice at Chorowait are not precisely *new*. Or, to put it another way, do not judge too harshly if certain of the theoretical bases that govern life at Chorowait are really rather old and unfashionable. After all, we did not construct our community with a view to mere novelty and innovation."

"On the other hand," Dalton of Chemistry said, "you should not condemn out of hand those features of our community that *are* novel and unusual. Bold improvisation has been needed to fulfil the various useful legacies of the past. And the willingness to use promising new combinations within the social body is what gives our work its greatest theoretical and practical value."

Other professors wanted to add a few words to assist Joenes's thinking. But Manisfree asked them all to stop. Joenes would see and judge for himself.

Only the irrepressible Blake felt called upon to say, "However you judge the experiment, Joenes, I'm sure there will be things to surprise you at Chorowait."

The professors chuckled appreciatively, then lapsed into

silence. Joenes was now more eager than ever to see their work, and his impatience grew during the long ride to the Adirondacks.

At last they were in the mountains, and Manisfree's old car wheezed and complained as it negotiated the rising hairpin turns. Then Blake touched Joenes on the shoulder and pointed. Joenes saw a high green mountain standing out from all the others. This he knew was Chorowait.

## HOW THE UTOPIA WORKED

Manisfree's car wearily climbed the deep-rutted road that led up the side of Chorowait Mountain. At the end of this road they came to a barrier constructed of logs. Here they left the car and proceeded on foot, first on a narrow dirt road, then on a path through the forest, and at last into the trackless forest itself, guided only by the steady upward trend of the land.

All of the professors were badly winded when, at last, they were greeted by two men from Chorowait.

These men were clad in deerskins. Each carried a bow and a quiver of arrows. They were tanned and ruddy, and they seemed to glow with abundant health and vitality. They contrasted strangely with the stooped, pale, hollow-chested professors.

Manisfree made the introductions. "This is Lunu," he said to Joenes, indicating the larger of the men. "He is the community leader. With him is Gat, whom none can excel at tracking."

Lunu addressed the professors in a language Joenes had never heard before.

"He is welcoming us," Dalton whispered to Joenes.

Gat added something.

"He says there are many good things to eat this month,"

Blake translated. "And he asks us to accompany him to the village."

"What language are they speaking?" Joenes asked.

"Chorowaitian," said Professor Vishnu of the Sanskrit Department. "It is an artificial language that we devised especially for the community, and for very important reasons."

"We are aware," said Manisfree, "that the qualities of a language tend to shape processes of thought, as well as to preserve ethnic and class stratifications. For these and other reasons, we considered it absolutely necessary to construct a new language for Chorowait."

"We had quite a time working it out," said Blake, with a reminiscent grin.

"Some of us wanted the utmost simplicity," Hanley of Anthropology said. "We wanted to maintain communication through a series of monosyllabic grunts, expecting that such a language would serve as a natural check to man's soaring and frequently destructive thoughts."

"Others among us," said Chandler of Philosophy, "wanted to construct a language of incredible complexity, with many distinct levels of abstraction. We felt this would serve the same purpose as the monosyllabic grunt, but would be more in keeping with man's needs."

"We had some jolly fights!" Dalton said.

"Finally," Manisfree said, "we decided to construct a language that would approximate the vowel frequency of Anglo-Saxon. The French Department didn't like this, of course. They wanted to use Early Provençal as a model; but we voted them down."

"Still, they had their influence," said Professor Vishnu. "Although we retained Anglo-Saxon vowel frequency, we used an Early Provençal pronunciation. But we discarded anything Indo-European in the construction of roots."

"The research was tremendous," Dalton said. "Thank

God Miss Hua was there to do the dogwork. It's a shame that girl is so ugly."

"These first-generation Chorowaitians are bilingual," Manisfree said, "but their children, or their children's children, will speak only Chorowaitian. I hope I live long enough to see that day. Already the effects of our new language on the community can be seen."

"Just consider," Blake said. "There are no words in Chorowaitian for 'homosexuality', 'rape', or 'murder'."

Lunu said, in English, "We call those things *Aleewadith*, which means thing-which-must-not-be-said."

"I think that shows," said Dalton, "the sort of thing that can be achieved through semantics."

Lunu and Gat led the way to the Chorowait village. Starting here, Joenes inspected Chorowait for the remainder of the day.

He saw that the community's homes had been constructed of birch bark and saplings. Women cooked over open fires, spun wool from the sheep they tended, and took care of babies. Men worked in the steep Chorowait fields, tilling the soil with wooden ploughs which they had fashioned. Other men hunted in the dense woods or fished in the icy Adirondack streams, bringing back deer and rabbit and trout, which they shared with the community.

In all of Chorowait, there was not a single manufactured article. Every tool had been fashioned there. Even the skinning knives were handmade, of iron dug from the ground of Chorowait. And what they could not make, the Chorowaitians did without.

Joenes observed all of this during the daylight hours, and commented favourably on the self-sufficiency, industry, and satisfaction which the community evidently possessed. But Professor Harris, who had accompanied him, seemed strangely apologetic about this aspect of Chorowait.

"You must understand, Joenes," Harris said, "that this

is the mere surface of Chorowait. To your eyes it must seem nothing but another dreary experiment in pastoral living."

Joenes had never seen nor heard of an experiment in pastoral living. He said that what he saw looked very good indeed.

"I suppose so," Harris said with a sigh. "But there have been countless numbers of these attempts. Many have started well, but few have continued well. Pastoral life has charming features, especially when educated, determined, and idealistic people undertake it. But such an existence is usually doomed to disillusion, cynicism and abandonment."

"Will this happen at Chorowait?" Joenes asked.

"We think not," Harris replied. "I hope we have learned from previous failures. After studying the utopian experiments of the past, we were able to build safeguards into our own community. In due time, you will see those safeguards."

That evening, Joenes ate a simple and rather unappetizing meal of milk, cheese, unleavened bread, and grapes. Then he was taken to the *Haierogu*, or place of worship. This was a clearing in the forest where the people worshipped the sun by day and the moon by night.

"Religion was quite a problem," Hanley whispered to Joenes as the multitude prostrated themselves in pale moonlight. "We didn't want to use anything associated with the Judeo-Christian tradition. Nor were we any fonder of Hinduism of Buddhism. In fact, after considerable research, nothing seemed very good. Some of us wanted to compromise on the T'iele deities of south-eastern Zanzibar; others favoured the Dhavagna Old Man, who is worshipped by an obscure offshoot of the Black Thai. But finally we agreed to deify the sun and moon. For one thing, there was ample historical precedent; and for another, we could represent this worship to the New York State authorities as a form of primitive Christianity."

"Was that important?" Joenes asked.

"Vastly! You'd be amazed how hard it is to get a licence for a place like this. We also had to prove that ours was a free-enterprise system. That presented some difficulties, since the community owns everything in common. Luckily, Gregorias was teaching Logic at the time, and he convinced the authorities."

The worshippers were swaying and moaning. An old man stepped forward, his face daubed with yellow clay, and began chanting in Chorowaitian.

"What is he saying?" Joenes asked.

Hanley said, "He is intoning a particularly lovely prayer that Geoffrard adapted from a Pindaric ode. This part goes:

'O Moon, in modesty decked in finest gossamer,
   Gliding with soft feet among the treetops of your people,
   Slipping behind the Acropolis out of fear of your fierce lover the Sun,
   Then touching with dewy fingers the white marble Parthenon,
   To you we sing this song.
   Craving your loving intercession to protect us
   From the menace of the dark hours,
   And to guard us for one little night
   From the Beast of all the world.'

"That's very pretty," Joenes said. "What does that part about the Acropolis and Parthenon mean?"

"Frankly," Harris said, "I'm not too sure of the suitability of that part myself. But the Classics Department

94

insisted upon having it in. And since Economics, Anthropology, Physics, and Chemistry had made most of the decisions up to then, we let them have their Parthenon. After all, there must be compromise in any co-operative venture."

Joenes nodded. "And what about that part about the menace of the dark hours, and the Beast of all the world?"

Harris nodded and winked. "Fear is necessary," he said.

Joenes was lodged for the night in a small cabin constructed entirely without nails. His bed of pine boughs was charmingly rustic, but also exceedingly uncomfortable. Joenes managed to adopt a posture that gave him the least pain, and to fall into a light doze.

He was awakened by the touch of a hand on his shoulder. Looking up, he saw an exceedingly pretty young woman bending over him with a tender smile on her face. Joenes was embarrassed at first, less for himself than for the woman, who he feared had come to the wrong cabin. But she showed him at once that she had made no mistake.

"I am Laka," she said. "I am the wife of Kor, who is the leader of the Young Men's Sun Association. I have come to sleep with you tonight, Joenes, and to do all in my power to welcome you to Chorowait."

"Thank you," Joenes said. "But does your husband know you're doing this?"

"What my husband knows or does not know is of little concern," Laka said. "Kor is a religious man, and a believer in the customs of Chorowait. It is a custom and a religious duty among us to make a guest welcome in this fashion. Didn't Professor Hanley tell you?"

Joenes replied that Hanley of Anthropology had not even hinted at this.

"Then he was having his little joke with you," Laka said.

95

"It was Professor Hanley himself who gave us this custom, which he took from some book."

"I had no idea," Joenes said, sliding over as Laka lay down on the pine boughs beside him.

"I've heard that Professor Hanley was quite vehement on this point," Laka said. "He met with some opposition from the Science Department. But Hanley held that if people needed religion, they also needed customs and practices; and that these customs and practices should be selected by an expert. Finally, that view prevailed."

"I see," Joenes said. "Did Hanley select other customs similar to this one?"

"Well," Laka said, "there's the Saturnalia, and the Bacchanalia, and the Eleusinian Mysteries, and the Festival of Dionysus, and Founder's Day, and the Spring and Fall Fertility Rites, and the Adoration of Adonis, and—"

Here Joenes interrupted and said that there seemed to be many holidays on Chorowait Mountain.

"Yes," Laka said. "It keeps us women exceedingly busy, but we've grown used to it. The men are not quite sure about it all. They dearly love the holidays, but they tend to grow jealous and spiteful when their own wives are involved."

"What do they do then?" Joenes asked.

"They follow the advice of Doctor Broign of the Psychology Department. They run for a prescribed distance of three miles through thick underbrush, then plunge into a cold stream and swim for a hundred yards, then beat upon a deerhide punching bag until utter exhaustion sets in. Utter exhaustion, Doctor Broign tells us, is always accompanied by a complete though temporary loss of emotionality."

"Does the doctor's prescription work?" Joenes asked.

"It seems to be infallible," Laka said. "If the cure is not completely successful the first time, a man simply has to

96

repeat it as often as necessary. The cure also has the virtue of improving the muscle tone."

"That's very interesting," Joenes said. Lying close to Laka, he suddenly found that he was no longer interested in anthropological discussions. For a fleeting moment he wondered if Hanley's imposition of his own tastes upon this community was not deplorable; but then he remembered that societies were always shaped by men, and that Hanley's tastes were no worse than some he had heard of, and much better than others. Resolving to think no more of the problem, Joenes reached out and touched Laka's dark hair.

Laka drew back from him with an involuntary shudder of revulsion.

"What's wrong?" Joenes asked. "Shouldn't I touch your hair?"

"It isn't that," Laka said. "The trouble is, I generally dislike being touched at all. Believe me, it has nothing to do with you. It's simply a part of my disposition."

"How extraordinary!" Joenes said. "And yet you came to this community willingly, and you remain here of your own free will?"

"That's true," Laka said. "It is a curious thing, but many civilized people who are attracted to a primitive existence have an aversion to the so-called pleasures of the body which the professors study with such great interest. In my own case, which is not atypical, I dearly love the mountains and the fields, and I rejoice in all practical work such as farming, fishing, or hunting. In order to have these things, I am willing to restrain my personal distaste for sexual experiences."

Joenes found this amazing, and he reflected upon the difficulties one encountered in populating a utopian community with people. His thoughts were interrupted by Laka, who had composed herself. With her feelings under careful restraint, she put her arms around Joenes's neck and drew him to her.

But now Joenes felt no more desire for her than he would for a tree or a cloud. Gently he pulled her hands away, saying, "No, Laka, I will not do violence to your natural tastes."

"But you must!" she cried. "It is the custom!"

"Since I am not a member of the community, I do not have to follow the custom."

"I suppose that's true," she said. "But all the other professors follow the custom, and then they argue the rights or wrongs of it later, in daylight."

"What they do is their own business," Joenes said, unmoved.

"It's my fault," Laka said. "I should have had better control over my feelings. But if you could only know how I have prayed for self-mastery!"

"I've no doubt of that," Joenes said. "But the offer of hospitality has been made, and thus the spirit of the custom has been kept. Remember that, Laka, and return now to your husband."

"I would be ashamed," Laka said. "The other women would know that something was wrong if I returned before daylight, and they would laugh at me. Also, my husband would be displeased."

"But doesn't he grow jealous and revengeful when you do this?"

"Of course he does," Laka said. "What kind of man would he be if he didn't? But he also has a great respect for learning, and a deep belief in the customs of Chorowait. Because of that. he insists that I take part in customs like this, even though it tears his heart apart to see me do so."

"He must be a very unhappy man," Joenes said.

"You're wrong, my husband is one of the happiest men

in the community. My husband believes that true happiness is spiritual, and that true spirituality can be acquired only through pain. So his pain makes him happy, or so he tells me. Also he follows Dr. Broign's prescription nearly every day, and has become the best runner and swimmer in the community."

Joenes hated to cause Laka's husband pain, even if that pain brought him happiness. But he also hated to cause Laka pain by sending her home. And he didn't want to cause himself pain by doing something that had become repugnant to him. There seemed no good way out of these difficulties, so Joenes told Laka to sleep in a corner of the cabin. That at least would spare her from being shamed in front of the other women.

Laka kissed him on the forehead with cold lips. Then she curled up on some pine boughs in the corner and went to sleep. Joenes found that sleep eluded him for a long time; but at last he dozed.

The events of that night were not finished, however. Joenes came suddenly awake in the small hours, alert and fearful, but with no idea of what had awakened him. The moon was down, and the darkness was at its most profound. Crickets, night birds, and small beasts of the forest had ceased all movement and all sound.

Joenes felt the skin along his spine prickle. He turned towards the door, certain that Laka's husband had come to kill him. Joenes had considered this possibility all night, since he had his doubts about Dr. Broign's prescription.

Then he realized that it was not an indignant husband who had shocked the night into silence. For now he heard a terrifying roar, of a fury and passion that could never have issued from a human throat. It stopped suddenly, and Joenes heard the movement of some huge creature in the underbrush outside.

"What is it?" Joenes asked.

Laka had risen to her feet, and she clung to Joenes as though all the strength had gone from her limbs. She whispered, "It is the Beast!"

"But I thought that was a myth," Joenes said.

"There are no myths on Chorowait Mountain," Laka said. "We worship the Sun and Moon, which are real. And we fear the Beast, which is just as real as a chipmunk. Sometimes we can placate the Beast, and sometimes we can drive it away. But tonight it comes to kill."

Joenes did not doubt any longer, especially when he heard the crash of an enormous body against the wall of the cabin. Although the wall was made of seasoned logs fastened with thongs and pegs, the logs were shattered by the impact of the Beast's body. And looking up, Joenes found himself staring full into the face of the Beast.

### THE BEAST OF THE UTOPIA

This creature was like nothing that Joenes had ever seen. In front it resembled a tiger, except that its massive head was black rather than tawny-striped. In the middle it was reminiscent of a bird, for rudimentary wings grew just below its shoulders. In back it was like a snake, possessing a tail that was twice as long as the Beast itself, as thick in its thickest part as a man's thigh, and scaled and barbed all over.

All of this Joenes saw in an instant, so strongly did the Beast impress itself upon his senses. When the Beast crouched to spring, Joenes scooped the fainting Laka in his arms and fled from the cabin. The Beast did not follow at once, but amused itself with a few minutes of wanton destruction before giving chase.

Joenes was able to join a group of village hunters. These

men, with Lunu at their head, stood with spears and arrows poised, ready to engage in battle against the Beast.

Standing nearby was the village witch doctor and his two assistants. The witch doctor's wrinkled old face was painted ochre and blue. In his right hand he held a skull, and with his left hand he poked frantically through a pile of magical ingredients. At the same time he was cursing his assistants.

"Idiots!" he was saying. "Criminally incompetent fools! Where is the moss from the dead man's head?"

"It is under your left foot, sir," one of the assistants said.

"What a place for it!" the witch doctor responded. "Give it here. Now where is the red shroud string?"

"In your pouch, sir," the other assistant answered.

The witch doctor drew it out and threaded it through the eye sockets of the skull. He bound the moss in the nose opening, then turned to his assistants

"You, Huang, I sent to read the stars; and you, Pollito, I sent to learn the message of the sacred golden deer. Tell me quickly and without delay what these messages were and what the gods request in order for us to stop the Beast tonight."

Huang said, "The stars told us to bind rosemary widdershins tonight."

The witch doctor seized a sprig of rosemary from his pile of ingredients and bound it to the skull with a shroud string, turning the string three times as the sun turns.

Pollito said, "The message of the sacred golden deer was to give the skull a pinch of snuff; that he said would be enough."

"Spare me your moronic rhyming," the witch doctor said, "and give me the snuff."

"I don't have it, sir."

"Then where is it?"

"Earlier you said that you had put the stuff in a safe place."

"Naturally. But in *which* safe place did I put it?" the witch doctor asked, rummaging wildly through his ingredients.

"Perhaps it's at the Underworld Altar," Huang said.

"Maybe it's at the Divining Place," Pollito said.

"No, none of those places seem right," the witch doctor said. "Let me think. . . ."

The Beast, however, gave him no further time for thought. It trotted out of Joenes's cabin and sprang at the line of hunters. A dozen arrows and spears darted forward to meet it, humming in the air like angry hornets. But these missiles had no effect. Unharmed, the Beast burst through the hunters' line. Already the witch doctor and his assistants had gathered up their ingredients and sprinted into the forest. The hunters also ran, but Lunu and two others were killed.

Joenes followed the hunters, and fear lent speed to his feet. At last he came to a clearing in the forest with a weathered stone altar in its centre. Here he found the witch doctor and his assistants, and behind them shuddered the hunters. In the forest, the howls of the Beast were growing louder.

The witch doctor was fumbling on the ground near the altar, saying, "I'm almost positive I put the snuff around here somewhere. I came here to ask the Sun's special blessing on it this afternoon. Pollito, do you remember what I did then?"

"I wasn't here," Pollito said. "You told us you were going to perform a secret rite, and that our presence was forbidden."

"Of course it was forbidden," the witch doctor said, digging vigorously around the altar with a stick. "But didn't you spy on me?"

"We would never do that," Huang said.

"Damned conformistic young morons!" the witch doctor said. "How do you expect to become witch doctors if you don't spy on me at every opportunity?"

The Beast appeared at the edge of the clearing, not fifty yards from the group. At the same moment the witch doctor bent down, then straightened up with a small deer-skin bag in his hand.

"Here it is, of course!" the witch doctor cried. "Right under the sacred ear of corn where I buried it this afternoon. Will one of you thumb-fingered imbeciles hand me another shroud string?"

Already Pollito was holding it out. With great dexterity, the witch doctor bound the bag to the skull's lower jaw, winding three times widdershins. Then he hefted the skull in his hand and said, "Is there anything I've forgotten? I don't think so. Now watch, you dull-witted bucolics, and see how the deed is done."

The witch doctor advanced on the Beast, holding the skull in both hands. Joenes, the hunters, and the two assistants, stood open-mouthed as the Beast pawed the earth into a trench three feet deep, stepped across it, and moved ominously towards the witch doctor.

The old man stepped close without a sign of fear. At the last moment he threw the skull, striking the Beast on the chest. It seemed a puny blow to Joenes; but the Beast let out an immense roar of pain, turned, and loped away into the forest.

The hunters were too weary to celebrate the Beast's defeat. They went silently to their cabins.

The witch doctor said to his assistants, "I hope you've had the sense to learn something from this. When skull exorcism is called for, the prepared skull, or *aharbitus*, must strike the centre of the Beast's chest. No other blow will do, but will simply augment the fury of the creature. Tomorrow we will study three-bodies exorcism, for which there is a very pretty ritual." Then he left.

Joenes lifted the still unconscious Laka and brought her back to his own cabin. As soon as the door was closed, Laka came to her senses and showered Joenes with kisses. Joenes pushed her away, telling her not to do violence to her feelings, nor to arouse his. But Laka declared that she was a changed woman, even if the change were only temporary. The sight of the Beast, she said, and of Joenes's bravery in rescuing her, had moved her to the depths of her being. Also, poor Lunu's death had shown her the value of passion in an ephemeral existence.

Joenes had his suspicions about these reasons, but there was no denying the fact that Laka had changed. Her eyes gleamed, and with a sudden leap reminiscent of the Beast's spring, she fell upon Joenes and toppled him on to the bed of pine boughs.

Joenes decided that, little as he knew of men, he knew even less of women. Also, the pine boughs hurt his back abominably. But soon he forgot his pain and his lack of knowledge. Both became exceedingly unimportant, and he did not think about them again until dawn flooded the cabin with light, and Laka slipped away to return to her own cabin.

### THE NECESSITY FOR
### THE BEAST OF THE UTOPIA

In the morning, Joenes met with his colleagues from the University. He told them his adventures of the previous night and expressed indignation at not having been warned about the Beast.

"But my dear Joenes!" said Professor Hanley. "We

wanted you to witness this vital facet of Chorowait for yourself, and to judge it without preconceptions."

"Even if that witnessing had cost me my life?" Joenes asked angrily.

"You were never in the slightest danger," Professor Chandler told him. "The Beast never attacks anyone connected with the University."

"It certainly seemed as though it was trying to kill me," Joenes said.

"I'm sure it *seemed* that way," Manisfree said. "But actually it was merely trying to get at Laka who, being a Chorowaitian, is a suitable victim for the Beast. You might have been jostled a bit when the Beast tore the girl from your arms; but that is the worst that could have happened to you."

Joenes felt chagrined at finding that his danger, which had seemed so dire the night before, was now revealed as no danger at all. To conceal his annoyance, he asked, "What sort of creature was it and to what species does it belong?"

Geoffrard of Classics cleared his throat importantly and said, "The Beast you saw last night is unique, and should not be confused with the Questing Beast whom Sir Pellinore pursued, nor with the Beasts of Revelation. The Chorowaitian Beast is more closely akin to the Opinicus, which the ancients tell us was part camel, part dragon, and part lion, though we do not know in what proportions. But even this kinship is superficial. As I said, our Beast is unique."

Joenes asked, "Where did this Beast come from?"

The professors looked at each other and giggled like embarrassed schoolboys. Then Blake of Physics controlled his mirth and said to Joenes, "The fact of the matter is, we ourselves gave birth to the Beast. We constructed it part by part and member by member, using the Chemistry Lab on week-ends and evenings. All departments of the

University co-operated in the design and fabrication of the Beast, but I should especially single out the contributions made by Chemistry, Physics, Mathematics, Cybernetics, Medicine, and Psychology. And I must also mention the contributions of Anthropology and Classics, whose inspiration this was. Special thanks are due to Professor Elling of Practical Arts who upholstered the entire Beast with the most durable of plastic skins. Nor should I forget Miss Hua, our student assistant, without whose careful collation of our notes the whole venture might have foundered."

The professors beamed happily at Blake's speech. Joenes, who had unwrapped a mystery only to find an enigma, still understood nothing.

Joenes said, "Let me see if I follow you. You *made* the Beast, constructing it out of ideas and inert matter in the Chemistry Lab?"

"That's very nicely put," Manisfree said. "Yes, that's exactly what we did."

"Was the Beast made with the knowledge of the University administration?"

Dalton winked and said, "You know how it is with those fellows, Joenes. They have an innate distaste for anything new, unless it's a gymnasium. So of course we didn't tell them."

"But they knew all the same," Manisfree said. "Administration always knows what's going on. But unless something is forced on their attention, they prefer to look the other way. They reason that a project like this might turn out well, in which case they and the University would get credit for farsighted wisdom. And if it turns out badly, they're safe because they knew nothing about it."

Several of the professors leaned forward with jokes about administrators on their lips. But Joenes spoke first, saying, "The construction of the Beast must have been very difficult."

"Indeed it was," said Ptolemy of Mathematics. "Excluding our own time, and the wear and tear on the Chem Lab, we had to spend twelve million four hundred thousand and twelve dollars and sixty-three cents on the fabrication of special parts. Hoggshead of Accounting kept a careful record of all expenses in case we should ever be asked."

"Where did the money come from?" Joenes asked.

"The government, of course," said Harris of Political Science. "I, and my colleague Finfitter of Economics, took over the problem of funds appropriation. We had enough left over to throw a victory banquet when Project Beast was completed. Too bad you weren't here for that, Joenes."

Harris forestalled Joenes's next question by adding, "Of course, we did not tell the government that we were building the Beast. Although they might still have granted funds, the inevitable bureaucratic delay would have been maddening. Instead, we said that we were working on a crash project to determine the feasibility of building an eight-lane coast-to-coast underground highway in the interests of national defence. Perhaps I do not need to add that Congress, which has always favoured highway construction, voted immediately and enthusiastically to give us funds."

Blake said, "Many of us felt that such a highway would be eminently practical, and perhaps extremely necessary. The more we thought about it, the more the idea grew on us. But the Beast came first. And even with government funds at our disposal, the task was tremendously difficult."

"Do you remember," asked Ptolemy, "the excruciating problems of programming the Beast's computer brain?"

"Lord yes!" Manisfree chuckled. "And what about the difficulties of giving it a parthenogenetic reproductive system?"

"Almost had us stopped," said Dalton. "But then, consider how we worked to co-ordinate and stabilize the Beast's movements! The poor thing lurched around the lab for weeks before we got that right."

"It killed old Duglaston of Neurology," Ptolemy said sadly.

"Accidents will happen," Dalton said. "I'm glad we were able to tell Administration that Duglaston had gone on his sabbatical."

The professors seemed to have a thousand anecdotes about the building of the Beast. But Joenes impatiently broke into their reminiscences.

"What I wanted to know," Joenes said, "is *why* you built the Beast?"

The professors had to think for a moment. They were separated by many years from the ecstatic days when they had first discovered the reasons for the Beast. But luckily, the reasons were all still there. After a slight pause, Blake said:

"The Beast was necessary, Joenes. It or something exactly like it was needed for the success of Utopian Chorowait, and by extension, for the fulfilment of the future which Chorowait represents."

"I see," Joenes said. "But why?"

"It's really terribly simple," Blake said. "Consider a society like Chorowait, or any other society, and ask yourself what caused its dissolution. It's a difficult question, and there really is no answer. But we can't be content with that. Men *do* live in societies; it seems to be in their nature. Given that as a necessary condition, we wanted to build an ideal societal model at Chorowait. Since all societies are breaking down today, we wanted ours to be stable, and as equitable as possible within a framework of accepted democratic law. We also wanted a pleasant society, and a meaningful one. Do you agree that these are worthwhile ideals?"

"Certainly," Joenes said. "But the Beast—"

"Yes, here is where the Beast comes in. The Beast, you see, is the implicit necessity upon which Chorowait rests."

Joenes looked confused, so Blake went on:

"It's actually a simple matter, and can be understood very readily. But first you must accept the need for stability, equitability within a framework of accepted law, and a meaning for existence. This you have accepted. Next you must accept the fact that no society can be made to operate on mere abstractions. When virtue goes unrewarded and vice is unpunished, men cease to believe, and their society falls apart. I'll grant you that men need ideals; but they cannot sustain them in the valueless void of the present world. With horror men discover how very far away the gods are, and how little difference anything makes."

"We will also grant you," Manisfree said, "that the fault undoubtedly lies in the individual man himself. Even though he is a thinking being, he refuses to think. Though possessed of intelligence, he rarely employs it for his own betterment. Yes, Joenes, I think we can accept all that."

Joenes nodded, amazed at these points the professors had granted him.

"So, given all that," Blake said, "we now see the absolute necessity of the Beast."

Blake turned away as though everything had been said. But Dalton, more zealous, continued:

"The Beast, my dear Joenes, is nothing less than Necessity personified. Today, with all mountains climbed and all oceans plumbed, with the planets within reach and the stars much too far away, with the gods gone and the state dissolving, what is there left? Man must pit his strength against something; we have provided the Beast for him. No longer must man dwell alone; the Beast is forever lurking nearby. No longer can man turn against himself in his idleness; he must be forever alert against the depredations of the Beast."

Manisfree said, "The Beast makes Chorowait society stable and cohesive. If the people did not work together, the Beast would kill them one by one. Only by the efforts of the entire populace of Chorowait is the Beast kept in reasonable check."

"It gives them a healthy respect for religion," Dalton said. "One needs religion when the Beast is on the prowl."

"It destroys complacency," Blake said. "No one could be complacent in the face of the Beast."

"Because of the Beast," Manisfree said, "the community of Chorowait is happy, family-oriented, religious, close to the soil, and continually aware of the necessity for virtue."

Joenes asked, "What stops the Beast from simply destroying the entire community?"

"Programming," Dalton said.

"I beg your pardon?'

"The Beast has been programmed, which is to say, certain information and responses have been built into its artificial brain. Needless to add, we took a great deal of care over that."

"You taught the Beast not to kill University professors?" Joenes said.

"Well, yes," Dalton answered. "We aren't too proud of that, to tell you the truth. But we thought we might be necessary for a while."

"How else is the Beast programmed?" Joenes asked.

"It is taught to seek out and destroy any ruler or ruling group of Chorowait people; next in priority to destroy the unvirtuous, and next to destroy any Chorowaitian. Because of that, any ruler must protect both himself and his people from the Beast. That in itself is quite enough to keep him out of mischief. But the ruler must also co-operate with the priesthood, without whose aid he is helpless. This serves as a decisive check to his powers."

"How can the priesthood help him?" Joenes asked.

"You yourself saw the witch doctor in action," Hanley said. "He and his assistants use certain substances that are gathered for them by the entire population of Chorowait. These, in proper combination, will turn the Beast back, since it is programmed to recognize and respond to the proper combination."

" Why can't the ruler simply take the substances and their combination, turn the Beast back himself, and rule without a priesthood? " Joenes asked.

"We took great care to preserve the separation between church and state," Harris said. "There is no single combination, you see, that will serve for all times the Beast appears. Instead, a vast quantity of formulae must be calculated each day, using lunar and stellar cycles, and variables such as temperature, humidity, wind speed, and the like."

"These calculations must keep the priests very busy," Joenes said.

"Indeed they do," Hanley said. "So busy that they have very little time in which to interfere with the affairs of the state. As a final safeguard against the possibility of a rich, complacent, and overweening priesthood, we have programmed a recurring random factor into the Beast. Against this nothing suffices, and the Beast will kill the witch doctor and no other. In that way, the witch doctor runs the same danger as does the ruler."

"But under those circumstances," Joenes said, "why would anyone want to be a priest or ruler? "

"Those are privileged positions," Manisfree said. "And as you saw, the humblest villager also runs the risk of death from the Beast. Since this is the case, men with ability will always accept the greater danger in order to exercise power, to fight against the Beast, and to enjoy greater privileges."

"You can see the interlocking nature of all this," Blake

said. "Both the ruler and the witch doctor maintain their positions only through the support of the people. An unpopular ruler would have no men to help him against the Beast, and would quickly be killed. An unpopular witch doctor would not receive the vital substances he needs in order to check the Beast, which must be gathered by the efforts of the entire people. Thus, both the ruler and the witch doctor hold power by popular consent and approval, and the Beast thus ensures a genuine democracy."

"There are some interesting sidelights on all this," said Hanley of Anthropology. "I believe this is the first time in recorded history that the full range of magical artifacts has been objectively necessary for existence. And it is probably the first time there has ever been a creature on Earth that partook so closely of the supernatural."

"In view of the dangers," Joenes said, "I don't see why any of your volunteers stay on Chorowait Mountain."

"They stay because the community is good and purposeful," Blake said, "and because they can fight against a palpable enemy instead of an unseen madman who works by perversity and kills through boredom."

"Some few of our volunteers had their doubts," Dalton said. "They weren't sure they could stick it out, even though we convinced them of the rightness of the thing. For the uncertain ones, Doctor Broign of Psychology was able to devise a simple operation on the frontal lobes of the brain. This operation didn't harm them in any way, and did not destroy intelligence and initiative like the terrible lobotomies of the past. Instead, it simply wiped out all knowledge of a world outside of Chorowait. With that accomplished, they had no other place to go."

"Was that ethical?" Joenes asked.

"They volunteered of their own free will," Hanley said. "And all we took from them was a little worthless knowledge."

"We didn't like to do it," Blake said. "But the pioneer stage of any society is often marked by unusual problems. Luckily, our pioneer stage is almost at an end."

"It ceases," Manisfree said, "when the Beast spawns."

The professors paused for a moment of reverent silence.

"You see," Ptolemy said, "we went to considerable difficulty to make the Beast parthenogenetic. Thus, self-fertilizing, its unkillable spawn will quickly spread to neighbouring communities. The offspring will not be programmed to stay within the confines of Chorowait Mountain, as the original Beast is. Instead, each will seek out and terrorize a community of its own."

"But other people will be helpless against them," Joenes said.

"Not for long. They will go to neighbouring Chorowait for advice, and will learn the formulae for controlling their own particular Beast. In this way the communities of the future will be born, and will spread over the face of the earth."

"Nor do we plan to leave it simply at that," Dalton said excitedly. "The Beast is all very well, but neither it nor its offspring are completely safe against man's destructive ingenuity. Therefore we have obtained more government grants, and we are building other creations."

"We will fill the skies with mechanical vampires!" Ptolemy said.

"Cleverly articulated zombies will walk the earth!" said Dalton.

"Fantastic monsters will swim in the seas!" said Manisfree.

"Mankind shall live among the fabulous creations it has always craved," Hanley said. "The griffin and the unicorn, the monoceros and the martikora, the hippogriff and the monster rat, all of these and many others will live. Superstition and fear will replace superficiality and boredom;

and there will be courage, too, in facing the djin. There will be happiness when the unicorn lays his great head in a virgin's lap, and joy when the Little People reward a virtuous man with a bag of gold! The greedy man will be infallibly punished by the coreophagi, and the lustful must beware of meeting the incarnate Aphrodite Pandemos. Man will no longer be alone in the universe, but will live with creatures as marvellous as himself. And he will live in accordance with the only rules his nature will accept— the rules that come from a supernatural made manifest upon the Earth! "

Joenes looked at the professors, and their faces glowed with happiness. Seeing this, Joenes did not ask if the rest of the world, outside of Chorowait, wanted this reign of the fabulous, or if they should perhaps be consulted about it. Nor did Joenes state his own impression, that this reign of the fabulous would be nothing more than a quantity of man-made machines built to act like the products of men's imaginations: instead of being divine and infallible, the machines would be merely mortal and prone to error, absurdly destructive, extremely irritating, and bound to be destroyed as soon as men had contrived the machinery to do so.

But it was not entirely a regard for his colleagues' feelings that stopped Joenes from saying these and other things. He also feared that such dedicated men might kill him if he showed a real spirit of dissent. Therefore he kept silent, and on the long ride back to the University he brooded on the difficulties of man's existence.

When they reached the University, Joenes decided that he would leave the cloistered life as soon as he possibly could.

## 10. HOW JOENES ENTERED THE GOVERNMENT

*(As told by Ma'aoa of Samoa)*

A N opportunity to leave the University came the following week when a government recruiter visited the campus. This man's name was Ollin, and his title was Under-secretary in Charge of Government Placement. He was a short man of perhaps fifty years, with close-cut white hair and a ruddy bulldog face. He gave an impression of dynamism and purpose that greatly affected Joenes.

Under-secretary Ollin made a short speech to the faculty: "Most of you know me, so I won't waste time with fancy words. I'll just remind you that the government needs talented and dedicated men for its various services and agencies. My job is to find those men. Anyone interested can visit me in room 222 of Old Scarmuth, which Dean Fols has graciously allowed me to use."

Joenes went there, and Under-secretary Ollin greeted him heartily.

"Take a seat," Ollin said. "Smoke? Drink? Glad to see someone turn up. I thought all you eggheads here at Stephen's Wood had your own plans for saving the world. Some sort of mechanical monster, isn't it?"

Joenes was amazed that Ollin knew about the Choro-wait experiment.

"We keep our eyes open," Ollin said. "It had us fooled at first because we thought it was just some gimmick for a monster movie. But now we know, and we've got FBI men on the case. Working undercover, they now make up one-third of the Chorowait group. We're going to move as soon as we've collected sufficient evidence."

"The mechanical Beast may spawn soon," Joenes said.

"It'll just give us more evidence," Ollin said. "Anyhow, let's direct out attention to you. I take it you're interested in government service?"

"I am. My name is Joenes, and I——"

"I know all that," Ollin said. He unlocked a large briefcase and removed a notebook.

"Let me see," he said, turning over the pages. "Joenes. Arrested in San Francisco for making an alleged subversive speech. Brought before a Congressional committee and judged an unco-operative and disrespectful witness, particularly in respect to your association with Arnold and Ronald Black, the twin Octagon spies. Tried by Oracle and given a ten-year suspended sentence. Spent a brief time in the Hollis Home for the Criminally Insane, then found employment at this University. During your time here you met daily with the founders of the Chorowait community."

Ollin closed the notebook and asked, "Is that more or less correct?"

"More or less," Joenes said, sensing the impossibility of argument or explanation. "I suppose my record renders me unfit for service in the government."

Ollin burst into hearty laughter. At last, wiping his eyes, he said, "Joenes, these surroundings must have made you a little soft in the head. There's nothing so terrible in your record. Your San Francisco speech is merely alleged, not proved. Your disrespect of Congress shows a lively sense of personal responsibility much like that of our greatest Presidents. There is inherent loyalty in your refusal to speak of Arnold and Ronald Black even to save yourself. Your conversion from communism is obvious; the FBI states that ever since your single misguided and naïve episode with the Blacks, you have steadfastly turned your back on the agents of international revolution. There is nothing shameful about your stay at the Hollis Home for the Criminally Insane; if you read the statistics, you would see that the majority of us need psychiatric care at some time or another. And there is nothing alarming about your association with Chorowait. Idealism can't always be channelled in the ways the government would like it to be. Even though we plan to stamp out Chorowait, we must approve the lofty though impractical planning that went into it. We in government aren't hypocrites, Joenes. We know that none of us is absolutely pure, and that every man has done some little thing he isn't exactly proud of. Judged in that way, you have really done nothing at all."

Joenes expressed his gratitude at the government's attitude.

"The man you can really thank," Ollin said, "is Sean Feinstein. In his capacity as Special Assistant to the Presidential Assistant, he put forth these views about you. We made a careful study of your case, and decided that you were the sort of man we wanted in government."

"Am I really?" Joenes asked.

"Past a doubt. We politicians are realists. We recognize the myriad problems that assail us today. To solve those problems we need the most daring, independent, fearless thinkers we can get. Nothing but the best will do, and no secondary considerations will stop us. We need men like *you*, Joenes. Will you enter the service of the government?"

"I will!" Joenes cried, aflame with enthusiasm. "And I will try to live up to the faith that you and Sean Feinstein have in me."

"I knew you'd say that, Joenes," Ollin said huskily. "They all do. I thank you from the bottom of my heart. Sign here and here."

Ollin presented Joenes with a standard government contract, and Joenes signed. The Under-secretary put the paper in his briefcase and shook Joenes warmly by the hand.

"Your position in the government starts as of this moment. Thank you, God bless you, and remember that we are all counting on you."

Ollin then started for the door, but Joenes called after him: "Wait! What is my job and where do I perform it?"

"You'll be notified," Ollin said.

"When? And by whom?"

"I'm only a recruiter," Ollin said. "What happens to the people I recruit is completely out of my jurisdiction. But don't worry, your assignment will come through like clockwork. Remember that we're counting on you. Now you must excuse me since I have a speaking engagement at Radcliffe."

Under-secretary Ollin left. Joenes was very excited about the possibilities before him, but a little sceptical about the speed with which the government would act.

The following morning, however, he received an official letter sent by special messenger. He was ordered to report to Room 432, East Wing, Portico Building, Washington, D.C., and to do so with the utmost dispatch. The letter was signed by no less a person than John Mudge, Special Assistant to the Services Co-ordination Chief.

Joenes took immediate leave of his colleagues, gazed for the last time on the green lawns and concrete paths of the University, and boarded the first jet for Washington.

It was a thrilling moment for Joenes when he arrived in the capital city. He walked down the rose marble streets towards the Portico Building, passing on his way the White House, seat of imperial American power. To his left was the great expanse of the Octagon, built to replace the smaller Pentagon. Beyond that were the Buildings of Congress.

These buildings were especially stirring to Joenes. For him they were the embodiment of the romance of history. The glory of Old Washington, capital of the Hellenic Con-Confederation before the disastrous Civil War, swam before his eyes. It was as though he could see the world-shaking debate between Pericles, representative of the marble-cutters' lobby, and Themistocles, the fiery submarine commander. He thought of Cleon, coming here from his home in Arcadian New Hampshire, putting forth his terse ideas about the prosecution of the war. The philosopher Alcibiades had lived here for a time, representing his native city of Louisiana, Xenophon had stood on these steps, and had been given a standing ovation for leading his ten thousand men all the way from the banks of the Yalu to the sanctuary of Pusan.

The memories crowded thick and fast! Here Thucydides wrote his definitive history of the tragic War Between the States. Hippocrates the Hellenic Surgeon General had conquered yellow fever here; and true to the oath he had devised, had never spoken of it. And here Lycurgus and Solon, the first judges of the Supreme Court, had held their famous debates on the nature of justice.

These famous men seemed to crowd around him as he crossed Washington's wide boulevards. Thinking of them, Joenes resolved to do his utmost, and to prove worthy of his ancestors.

In this ecstatic frame of mind, Joenes arrived at Room 432 of the East Wing of the Portico Building. John Mudge, the Special Assistant, made him welcome without delay. Mudge was kind and affable, unhurried in spite of his huge work load. Joenes learned that Mudge made all policy decisions in the Services Co-ordination Office, since his superior spent his days and nights penning useless petitions for transfer to the Army.

"Well, Joenes," Mudge said, "you've been assigned to us, and we're very glad to have you. I think I should explain immediately what this office does. We operate as an inter-Service agency designed to avoid duplication of effort between the semi-autonomous forces of the military. Aside from that, we also serve as an intelligence and information agency for all Service programmes, and as a governmental policy planner in the fields of military, psychological, and economic warfare."

"That sounds like quite a lot," Joenes said.

"It is far too much," Mudge answered. "And yet, our work is absolutely necessary. Take our primary task of co-ordination between the Services. Only last year, before this office was formed, elements of our Army fought a three-day battle in the deepest jungles of northern Thailand. Imagine their chagrin when the smoke cleared and they found that they had been attacking a strongly entrenched battalion of U.S. Marines! Imagine the effect upon service morale! With our military obligations stretched so thinly across the globe, and so intricately disposed, we must be forever vigilant against incidents of this kind."

Joenes nodded in agreement. Mudge went on to explain the necessity for their other duties.

"Take intelligence, for example," Mudge said. "At one time that was the special province of the Central Intelligence Agency. But today, CIA refuses to release its information, requesting instead that it be given more troops to deal with the problems it uncovers."

"Deplorable," Joenes said.

"And of course the same holds true in greater degree for Army Intelligence, Navy Intelligence, Air Force Intelligence, Marine Corps Intelligence, Space Corps Intelligence, and all the others. The patriotism of the men of these Services cannot be doubted; but each, having been given the means of waging independent warfare, considers his Service the only one in a position to judge the danger and prosecute the conflict to a conclusion. This state of affairs renders any information on the enemy contradictory and suspect. And this in turn paralyzes the government because it has no reliable information upon which to plan policy."

"I had no idea the problem was so severe," Joenes said.

"It is severe and insoluble," Mudge replied. "To my way of thinking, the fault lies in the very size of the governmental organization, which has swollen past all precedent. A scientist friend of mine once told me that an organism that grows beyond its natural size tends to break up into its component parts, eventually to begin the growing process all over again. We have grown too huge, and fragmentation has set in. Yet our growth was a natural consequence of the times, and we cannot allow any break-up to occur as yet. The Cold War is still upon us, and we must patch and mend and hold our Services in some semblance of order and co-operation. We in Co-ordination must discover the truth about the enemy, present this truth to the government as policy, and induce the Services to act upon this policy. We must persevere until the external danger is past, and then hope to reduce the size of our bureaucracy before the forces of chaos do the job for us."

"I think I understand," Joenes said. "And I am in full accord."

"I knew you would be," Mudge replied. "I knew it from the time I read your dossier and requested your appointment here. I told myself that this man would be a natural co-ordinator, and in spite of many difficulties I had you cleared for government service."

"But I thought that was the work of Sean Feinstein," Joenes said.

Mudge smiled. "Sean is little more than a figurehead who signs the papers we put in front of him. He is also a first-class patriot, having volunteered for the secret but necessary role of government scapegoat. In Sean's name we make all dubious, unpopular, or questionable decisions. When they turn out well, the Chiefs take the credit. When they turn out badly, Sean takes the blame. In this way, the usefulness of the Chiefs is not impaired."

"It must be very hard on Sean," Joenes said.

"Of course it is. But perhaps Sean would not be happy if things were not very hard on him. So a psychologist friend of mine believes. Another psychologist of my acquaintance, of a more mystical turn of mind, believes that Sean Feinstein is fulfilling an obligatory historical function, that he is destined to be a prime mover of men and events, a crucial figure in all histories, and a vital force in the enlightenment of the people; and that for these reasons he is detested and reviled by the populace he serves. But wherever the truth lies, I find Sean an extremely necessary person."

"I would like to meet him and shake his hand," Joenes said.

"That will not be possible just yet," Mudge said. "Sean is presently serving a term of solitary confinement upon a diet of bread and water. He was found guilty of stealing 24 atomic howitzers and 187 atomic grenades from the U.S. Army."

"Did he actually steal those things?" Joenes asked.

"Yes. But he did so at our request. We armed a Signal Corps detachment with them, and they succeeded in winning the Battle of Rosy Gulch in south-eastern Bolivia. The Signal Corps, I might add, had long requested those weapons in vain."

"I am very sorry for Sean," Joenes said. "What is his sentence?"

"Death," said Mudge. "But he will be pardoned. He always is. Sean is too important not to be pardoned."

Mudge looked away for a moment, then turned back to Joenes. "Your particular work," he said, "will be of the utmost importance. We are sending you to Russia on a tour of inspection and analysis. Many such inspections have been made in the past, of course. But either they have been made from the bias of one Service, in which case they are worthless, or they have been made from a Co-ordinated standpoint, in which case they have been marked Top Secret and filed unread in the Top Secret room beneath Fort Knox. I have my chief's assurance, and I give you mine, that no such fate will befall your report. It will be read and acted upon. We are determined to impose Co-ordination, and anything you say about the enemy will be accepted and utilized. Now, Joenes, you will receive a full clearance, then a briefing, then orders."

Mudge took Joenes to Security Division, where a colonel in charge of Phrenology felt his head for suspicious bumps. After that, Joenes ran the gauntlet of government astrologists, card-readers, tea-leaf readers, physiognomists, psychologists, casuists, and computers. At the end he was declared loyal, sane, responsible, trustworthy, reverent, and above all, lucky. On the basis of this he was given a Portmanteau Clearance and allowed to read classified documents.

We have only a partial list of the papers Joenes read in the grey iron Secrets Room, with two armed guards standing beside him, blindfolded to make sure they would not inadvertently glance at the precious documents. But we know that Joenes read:

"The Yalta Papers," which told of the historic meeting

123

between President Roosevelt, Czar Nicholas II, and Emperor Ming. Joenes learned how the fateful decisions made in Yalta affected present-day politics; and he learned of the violent opposition to those decisions that was voiced by Don Winslow, the Supreme Naval Commander.

Next he read, "I was a Male War Bride," a devastating exposé of unnatural practices in the Armed Services.

And he also read the following:

"Little Orphan Annie Meets Wolf Man," a detailed espionage manual written by one of the most accomplished female spies who ever lived.

"Tarzan and the Black City," an extraordinary account of commando activities in Russian-held East Africa.

"The Cantos," author unknown, a cryptic statement of the enemy's monetary and racial theories.

"Buck Rogers Enters Mungo," a documentary account of the latest exploit of the Space Corps, illustrated.

"First Principles," by Spencer, "The Apocrypha," author unknown, "The Republic," by Plato, and "Maleus Malificarum," jointly authored by Torquemada, Bishop Berkeley, and Harpo Marx. These four works were the soul and spearhead of Communist doctrine, and we can be sure that Joenes read them with great profit.

Of course he also read "The Playboy of the Western World," by Immanuel Kant, which was the definitive refutation of the above-mentioned Communist works.

All of these documents have been lost to us, due to the unfortunate circumstance of their having been written on paper instead of learned by heart. We would give much to know the substance of those works that shaped the brilliant and erratic politics of the times. And we cannot help but ask whether Joenes read the few twentieth-century classics that have come down to our own time. Did he peruse the stirring *Boots*, cast in enduring bronze. Did he read *The Practical Man's Guide to Real Estate*, that monumental fantasy that, almost single-handed, shaped the temper of the twentieth century? Did Joenes ever meet the venerable Robinson Crusoe, his contemporary, greatest of the twentieth-century poets? Did he speak with any of the member of the Swiss Family Robinson, whose sculptures can be seen in many of our museums?

Alas, Joenes never spoke of these cultural things. Instead, his accounts focus upon matters of far greater concern to his beleaguered age.

So it was that Joenes, after reading steadily for three days and three nights, arose and left the grey iron Secrets Room and its blindfolded guards. He was now fully cognizant of the state of the nation and of the world. With high hopes and dire forebodings he opened his orders.

These orders instructed him to report to Room 18891, Floor 12, Level 6, Wing 63, Subsection AJB2, of the Octagon. With the orders was a map to aid him find his way around the massive structure. When he should reach Room 18891, a high Octagon official known only as Mr. M. would give him his final instructions and arrange his departure on a special jet for Russia.

Joenes's heart filled with joy when he read these orders, for at last he had a chance to play a part in great affairs. He rushed off to the Octagon to receive his final instructions and be off. But the duty Joenes wished to perform was not so easily captured.

*(The Octagon Adventures and the four stories that comprise it are told by Maubingi of Tahiti)*

AFIRE with anticipation, Joenes entered the Octagon. He stared around him for a moment, never having imagined that so enormous and majestic a building could exist. Then, recovering, he walked swiftly down great halls and corridors, up stairways, through bypasses, across lobbies, and down more corridors.

By the time his first flush of enthusiasm had worn off, he was able to see that his map was hopelessly incorrect, for its various designations bore no reference to anything he saw around him. It seemed, in fact, to be a map of another building. Joenes was now deep in the heart of the Octagon, unsure of the way that lay ahead, dubious of his ability to retrace his footsteps. Therefore he put the map in his pocket and decided to ask advice of the first person he met.

Soon he overtook a man walking down the corridor. This man wore the uniform of a colonel in the Cartography Department, and his bearing was kindly and distinguished.

Joenes stopped the colonel, explaining that he was lost and that his map seemed to be useless.

The colonel glanced at Joenes's map and said, "Oh, yes, that's perfectly in order. This map is our Octagon Series A443-321B, which my office published only last week."

"But it doesn't tell me anything," Joenes said.

"You're damned right it doesn't," the colonel answered

proudly. "Do you have any idea how important this building is? Did you know that every top government agency, including the most secret ones, are housed here?"

"I know that the building is very important," Joenes said. "But——"

"Then you can understand the position we would be in," the colonel went on, "if our enemies really understood the building and its offices. Spies would infiltrate these corridors. Disguised as soldiers and congressmen, they would have access to our most vital information. No security measures could hope to restrain a cunning and determined spy armed with information like that. We would be lost, my dear sir, utterly lost. But a map like this, which is most confusing to a spy, is one of our most important safeguards."

"I suppose it is," Joenes said politely.

The colonel of Cartography touched Joenes's map lovingly and said, "You have no idea how difficult it is to make such a map."

"Really?" Joenes said. "I would have thought it quite simple to construct a map of an imaginary place."

"The layman always thinks that. Only a fellow mapmaker, or a spy, could appreciate our problems. To construct a map that tells nothing and yet seems true, giving even an expert the sensation of verisimilitude—that, my friend, requires art of the highest order!"

"I'm sure it does," Joenes said. "But why do you bother making a false map at all?"

"For the sake of security," the colonel said. "But to understand that, you must know how a spy thinks when he gets a map like this; then you would see how this map strikes directly at the spy's greatest weakness, rendering him more ineffectual than no map at all would do. And to understand all that, you must comprehend the mentality of a spy."

Joenes admitted that he was bewildered by this explanation. But the colonel said it was merely a matter of understanding the nature of a spy. And to illustrate this nature, he then told Joenes a story about a spy, and how he behaved when he was in possession of the map.

### THE STORY OF THE SPY

The spy (said the colonel) has overcome all previous obstacles. Armed with the precious map, he has penetrated deep into the building. Now he tries to use the map, and sees at once that it doesn't represent the thing he seeks. But he also sees that the map is beautifully made and expensively printed on government paper; it bears a government serial number and a countersigned stamp of approval. It is a clear, lucid map, a triumph of the mapmaker's skill. Does the spy throw it away and attempt to draw the bewildering complexities around him on a wretched little pocket pad, using only a ball-point pen that doesn't work very well? He most assuredly does not. Even though ultimate success might lie in that direction, our spy is only human. He does not wish to match his puny ability at visualizing, abstracting, drawing and generalizing, against experts in the field. It would take the highest courage and self-confidence for him to throw away this magnificent map and proceed with nothing but his senses to guide him. If he had the necessary qualities to do that, he would never have been a spy in the first place. He would have been a leader of men, or perhaps a great artist or scientist. But he is none of these things; he is a spy; which is to say, a man who has chosen to find out about things rather than to do things, and to discover what others know rather than to search for what he knows. Necessarily he assumes the existence of truths external to himself, since no real spy could believe that his lifework was to discover frivolous falsehoods.

This is all very important when we consider the character of any spy, and especially of the spy who has stolen a government map and penetrated deep into this closely guarded building.

I think we might fairly call this spy both genuine and excellent, and imbued with extraordinary dedication, cunning, and perseverance. These qualities have brought him past all dangers to a place of vantage within the building. But these very qualities also tend to shape his thoughts, making certain actions possible and others not. So we must realize that the better he is at his work, the more superb his guile, the stronger his dedication, the longer his experience, the greater his patience, then the less able he is to put aside these virtues, throw away the map, take a pen and blank paper in hand, and scribble down what he sees. Perhaps the idea of discarding an official government map sounds simple to you; but the spy finds this concept distasteful, foreign, repugnant, and utterly alien to his genius.

Instead, the spy begins to reason about the map in spy-fashion, which he thinks is the only way there is of reasoning, but which we know is merely a way he has of evading a discrepancy that life has made manifest, but which instinct and reason reject.

Here is a genuine government issue map, and over there are various corridors and doorways. The spy looks at the map, that document similar to other true and valuable documents he has risked his life to steal. He asks himself, "Can this map be false? I know that it issues from the government, and I know that I stole it from an official who evidently prized it and thought it valuable. Am I justified in ignoring this document simply because it seems to have no bearing on what I see around me?'

The spy ponders this question, and at last comes up with the operative word: "seems". The map only *seems* to have no bearing! Appearance had momentarily deceived him. He was nearly led astray by the testimony of his senses. The makers of the map almost did this to *him*, a master of tricks and disguises, a man who has spent a lifetime in worming out their secrets. Of course, it is all explicable now.

The spy says, "They tried to fool me with my own tricks! Clumsily, of course, but at least they are beginning to think in the right way."

By this the spy means that they are beginning to think as he does, thereby making their secrets more comprehensible to him. This pleases him. His bad humour, brought on by the lack of conformity between the map and the building, has now completely vanished. He is cheerful, energetic, prepared for any difficulty, ready to pursue this problem to its ultimate conclusion.

"Let me consider the facts and their implications," says the spy. "First, I know this map is important. Everything about it, and everything I have ever experienced, leads me to that premise. I also know that the map does not *seem* to represent the building it is supposed to represent. Quite obviously there is a relationship of some kind between the map and the building. What is this relationship, and what is the truth about the map?"

The spy thinks for a moment, then says, "The implication points to a cipher, a mystification that some skilled and cunning craftsman wove into the map, which the people for whom the map is intended know about, but which I hitherto did not know about."

After saying this, the spy draws himself to his full height and adds, "I, however, have spent a lifetime in the solving of ciphers. Indeed, there is nothing I am quite so interested in as ciphers. One might say that I was shaped by destiny to solve ciphers, and that destiny has conspired with chance to put me here, now, with this crucial coded document in my hand."

Our spy feels exalted. But then he asks himself, "Am I not being dogmatic in insisting, at the very start of my investigation, that this document is a true ciphered map and no other thing? Experience has taught me the painful lesson that men are capable of devious thinking. I myself am the living proof of that, for my cunning ways of thinking and acting have enabled me to remain hidden in the midst of my enemies, and to discover many of their secrets. Remembering that, don't I do them an injustice not to allow them the possibility of similar cunning?

"Very well," the spy says. "Even though reason and instinct tell me that the map is true in every respect, and misleading only because I do not have the key to the cipher, I must admit the possibility of it being false in part, and therefore true only in part. There are good reasons one could give for this assumption. Suppose the true part of the map is the only part that was needed by the official I stole it from. He, armed with a prior knowledge I do not have, would follow only the part that is true and pertinent to his work. Being the dull civil servant he is, and above all being uninterested in maps and ciphers, he would simply follow the true part to his office, and would ignore the false part. The map itself, with its false section joined so cleverly to the true would not bother him. And why should it? His work has nothing to do with maps. He has no more interest in the truth or falseness of the map than I have in the details of his petty job. Like me, he has no time to worry about complicated matters that do not concern him. He can use the map without doing violence to his feelings."

The spy is amused and saddened when he thinks of this man, using the map but having no interest in it.

How strange people are! How odd that the official merely made use of the map, but never questioned its mysterious nature; while the spy knows that the only important matter is a complete understanding of the map and what it represents. From this understanding all other things will flow and the secrets of the entire building will be accessible. This seems so obvious to him that he can't understand the official's lack of concern with the map. The spy's own interest seems to him so natural, so necessary, so universal, that he is almost led to believe that the official is not human, but is rather a member of some other species.

"But no," he tells himself. "It may feel that way, but the real difference between the official and me probably lies in heredity, or in environmental influences, or something like that. I must not let it disturb me. I have always known how strange and unknowable human beings are. Even spies, the most easily understood people in the world, have different methods and hold different attitudes. Yes, it is a strange world, and I have very little knowledge of it. What do I know of history, psychology, music, art, or literature? Oh, I could hold a sensible conversation on those subjects, but deep in my heart I know that I know nothing about them."

The spy is unhappy about this. But then he thinks, "Luckily, there *is* one thing I do understand. That is spying. No man can do everything, and I have done very well to become the expert I am in my own field. In that expertness lies my hope and my salvation. In that very narrowness lies my true depth, and my yardstick with which to test the world. After all, I know a great deal about the history and psychology of spying, and I have read most of the literature of spying. I have looked at the famous paintings of spies, and have frequently heard the well-known opera about spies. Thus, my depth gives me breadth. My deep knowledge of this one thing gives me a firm base in the world. I can stand upon that base and look at other matters with a certain perspective.

"Of course," the spy reminds himself, "I must never make the error of thinking that all things can be reduced to a matter of spying and its techniques. Even if this appears to be the case, it is the sort of simplification an intelligent man must avoid. No, spying is not everything! It is merely the key to everything."

Having established that, the spy goes on to say, "Spying is *not* everything; but luckily for me, this matter of the map does concern spying. Maps are the very heart of spying, and when I hold a map in my hand and know that the government made it, then I am dealing with a problem for which I have a special competency. A map in cipher is of particular concern to spying, as is a map that is partially false. Even a map that was wholly false would necessarily concern spying."

Now the spy is ready to analyze the map. He tells himself, "There are three possibilities. First, the map is true, and in cipher. In that case, I must decode it, using all my patience and skill.

"Second, the map is only partially true, and in cipher. In that case I will determine which is the true part, and then decode it. That might seem difficult to a person who knows nothing about the work; but to the expert it is the sort of difficulty that can be overcome. And as soon as I have decoded the tiniest fraction of the map's true portion, all the rest will open for me. That would leave the false portion, which someone else might throw away. But I would not. I would treat the false portion exactly as I would treat the entire map if it were false, which is possibility number three.

"Third, if the entire map is false, I must see what kind of information I can extract from that falseness. Granted that the idea of a false government map is absurd, let's say that is the case. Or rather, let's say that falseness was the *intention* of the makers of the map. In such a case I would have to ask, how does one draw a false map?

"It is no easy matter, that I know. If the mapmaker works in this building, moves up and down its corridors, steps into and out of its offices, then he knows the building as no other person could. If this man tries to draw a false map, how can he avoid inadvertently drawing some portion of the true building?

"He can't, really. The truth in which he is steeped would render his quest for absolute falseness impossible. And if by accident he drew any portion of the true map, I could infallibly find that true part, and all of the building's jealously guarded security would be as nothing.

"But let's assume that the high officials are aware of all this and have given careful study to the problem of constructing a false map. Let's give them the benefit of every doubt within the necessities of the situation. They know that the map, in order to serve its purpose, must be drawn by a skilled mapmaker who will make it conform to the logical rules for maps and for buildings; and that the map must be false, and not true even inadvertently.

"To solve the problem, let us say that the high officials find a civilian mapmaker who has no knowledge of the building. He is brought to the place blindfolded, given a carefully guarded office, and told to draw a map of an imaginary building. He does so; but the problem of inadvertent truth still remains. Therefore, a government mapmaker who *does* know the truth must check the map. The government mapmaker checks (and no person but a mapmaker would be competent to judge), and he says that this map is excellent since it is entirely false.

"In that ultimate case, the map is still nothing but a cipher! It has been drawn by a skilled civilian mapmaker, and thus conforms to the general principles that govern the drawing of maps. It is of a building, and conforms to the rules for drawing buildings. It has been judged false; but it has been judged so by an official mapmaker *who knew the truth*, and was able to decide about every detail of the map on the basis of his knowledge of the true building. The so-called false map, then, is merely a sort of reversed or distorted image of the truth known by the official mapmaker; and the relationship between the true building and the false map has been established through his judgment, since he knew both true and false and judged their dissimilarity. His necessarily intermediary judgment demonstrates the nature of the false map— which, being a logical distortion that conceals the truth, may be called a cipher!

"And since this cipher follows the accepted rules for maps and buildings, it is susceptible to cipher analysis!"

This completes the spy's analysis of the three possibilities of the map, all of which can now be reduced to one: that the map is true, and in cipher.

Dazed by this discovery, the spy says, "They thought they could trick me, but it cannot be done in my chosen field. In my search for truth, I have lived all my life by falsehood and deceit; but I have always known my own reality. Because of myself and my search, I above all men know that there is no such thing as falsehood, and that everything is either the truth or a cipher. If it is the truth, I follow it; and if it is a cipher, I solve it. A cipher, after all, is merely a concealed truth!"

At last the spy is happy. He has moved through the deepest perplexities, and has had the courage to face the most terrible possibilities. His reward is now before him.

For now, paying strict attention to the map, and holding that well-made creation with loving care, the spy begins the task that is the culmination of his life, and which eternity would not give him time enough to complete. He begins his attempt to decipher the false map.

### THE MAPMAKER'S EXPLANATION

When the colonel had finished, he and Joenes stood silent for a while. Then Joenes said, "I can't help feeling sorry for that spy."

"It was a sad story," the colonel said. "But then, all men's stories are sad."

"If the spy is caught, what will his punishment be?"

"He has already imposed it upon himself," the colonel replied. "His punishment is to decipher the map."

Joenes could think of no worse fate. He asked, "Do you catch many spies here in the Octagon?"

"To date," the colonel said, "not a single spy has succeeded in passing our outer security measures and penetrating into the building proper."

The colonel must have noticed a look of disappointment on Joenes's face, for he added quickly, "That, however, does not invalidate my story. If a spy did get in here in spite of all security, he would behave just as I told you. And believe me, spies are caught every week in the network of outer defences."

"I didn't notice any defences," Joenes said.

"Of course not. For one thing, you aren't a spy. For another, security knows its work well enough not to reveal its presence, but only to act when necessary. That is how matters stand at present. For the future, when more cunning spies are born, we in Cartography have our false maps."

Joenes nodded. He was eager now to continue his own job, but unsure how to go about it. Deciding on indirection,

136

he asked the colonel, "Are you convinced that I am not a spy?"

"Everyone is a spy to some extent," the colonel said. "But in regard to the special meaning you imply, yes, I am quite convinced that you are not a spy."

"Well then," Joenes said, "I must tell you that I am under special orders to go to a certain office here."

"May I see those orders?" the colonel asked. Joenes handed them over. The colonel studied the orders and gave them back.

"They seem official," the colonel said. "You should certainly go to that office at once."

"That is my problem," Joenes said. "The truth is, I'm lost. I tried to follow one of your excellent false maps, and naturally enough I found nothing at all. Since you know I'm not a spy, and also know that I'm on official business, I would appreciate any assistance you could give me."

Joenes had made this request in a careful and round-about way, which he thought would be most suitable to the colonel's mentality. But the colonel looked away with a look of embarrassment on his dignified features.

"I'm very much afraid I can't help you," the colonel said. "I do not have the faintest idea where your office is, and I don't even know what direction to recommend."

"But that's impossible!" Joenes cried. "You are a cartographer, an official mapmaker of this building. And even though you draw false maps, I'm sure you also draw true ones, since that must be in your nature."

"All that you say is correct," the colonel said. "Especially that last about my nature. Anyone can deduce the nature of a cartographer, since his nature resides in his work. That work is to draw maps of the most exacting accuracy, maps so precise and lucid that the dullest of men could follow them. My function has been perverted by necessities beyond my control, so I must spend much of my time drawing false maps that give the appearance of truth. But as you have guessed, nothing can stop a genuine map-maker from drawing genuine maps. I would do it even if it were forbidden. And luckily, it is not forbidden. It is expressly commanded."

"By whom?" Joenes asked.

"By the high officials of this building," the colonel said. "They control security, and they use the true maps to aid them in disposing their forces. But of course, the true maps are a mere convenience for them, a bit of paper they refer to as casually as you would glance at your watch to see whether it was three-thirty or three-forty. If necessary they could do without the maps entirely, relying on their knowledge and power. They might find it an annoyance, but not a serious one."

"If you draw true maps for them," Joenes said, "surely you can tell me where to go now."

"I can't," the colonel said. "Only the high officials know the building well enough to go where they want to."

The colonel saw Joenes's look of disbelief. He said, "I know how unreasonable all this must sound to you. But you see, I draw only one section of the building at a time; no other method would work since the building is so vast and so complex. I draw my section and send it to a high official by messenger, and later I draw another section, and so on. Perhaps you think I could combine my knowledge of the various parts and know the whole? I tell you at once that I cannot. For one thing, there are other cartographers who draw parts of the building that I never have time to see. But even if I mapped the entire structure by myself, piece by piece, I could never combine all those pieces into an understandable unity. Any one portion of the building seems comprehensible to me, and I represent it with great accuracy on paper. But when it comes to under-

138

standing all the countless sections I have mapped, then I become confused, I can't tell one part from the other. And if I think about it for very long my sleep and appetite are affected, I smoke too much, I find solace in drink, and my work suffers. Sometimes, when these bad spells are on me, I make inaccuracies, and I do not perceive my errors until the officials send that portion of the map back for revision. This shakes my faith in my own proven abilities; I determine to end my bad habits and stick to my task of skilful portrayal of one section at a time, not bothering my head about the whole."

The colonel paused and rubbed his eyes. "As you may expect," he went on, "my good resolves don't last for long, especially when I am in the company of my fellow carto-cartographers. At those times we sometimes discuss the building and try to determine among us what it really is. Usually we cartographers are shy men; like spies, we prefer to do our work in solitude and not to discuss it with each other. But the solitude we love can become overwhelming; and then we overcome the limits of our nature and talk about the building, each of us adding his increment of knowledge eagerly and without jealousy, all of us bent upon understanding the whole building. But those are the times that prove the most discouraging."

"Why is that?" Joenes asked.

"As I told you," the colonel said, "our map sections are sometimes sent back for revision, and we assume that we have made mistakes even though there is never any official comment. But when we mapmakers talk together, we occasionally find that two of us have mapped the same section, each remembering and drawing it differently. That sort of human error is to be expected, of course. But what is disconcerting is when the high officials accept both versions. You can imagine a mapmaker's sensations when he learns something like that!"

"Do you have any explanation for it?" Joenes asked.

"Well, for one thing, mapmakers have their individual styles and idiosyncrasies, and that might account for the discrepancy. For another, even the best of memories is untrustworthy, so we might not have mapped the same section. But to my way of thinking these explanations are not sufficient, and only one thing makes sense."

"What's that?" Joenes asked.

"I believe that workmen, under orders from the high officials, are continually changing portions of the building. It is the only explanation that satisfies me. I have even caught glimpses of what could only be workmen. But even if I hadn't seen them, I would still believe it. Just consider. The high officials are concerned with security, and the finest security possible would be to keep the building in a constant state of change. Next, if the building were static, a single mapmaking survey would be sufficient, instead of the continual drawing and revising we are called upon to do. Finally, the high officials are trying to control a complex and ever-changing world; therefore as the world changes, so must the building. More offices must be built, and old ones have to be altered for new tenants; a row of cubicles must be removed and an auditorium put in its place; whole corridors must be closed down to allow the installation of new wiring and plumbing. And so forth. Some of these changes are extremely evident. Any man can see them, not only a mapmaker. But other changes are made apparently in secrecy, or in parts of the building I do not visit until the work is completed. Then the new looks bafflingly like the old, although I can still sense a difference. It is for those reasons that I believe the building is continually being changed, thus rendering a complete knowledge of it impossible."

"If this place is as unknowable as you say it is," Joenes

140

said, "then how do you find your way back to your own office?"

"There, I am ashamed to say, my mapmaking skill does not help me. I find my office just as everyone else here finds his office—by something that resembles instinct. The other workers don't know this; they think they find their way by some process of the intelligence, some kind of a turn-right turn-left system. Like the spy, they believe they could learn anything about the building if they wanted to. It would make you laugh or cry to hear the statements these people make about this building, even though they have never ventured beyond the corridor that leads to their office. But I, a mapmaker, wander all over the building in my work. Sometimes great changes occur in territory I have already passed, rendering it unrecognizable. Then something that is not knowledge guides me back to my office, exactly as it guides the office workers."

"I see," Joenes said, though he was actually very confused. "So you really don't know what I should do in order to find this office?"

"I really do not know."

"Could you give me any advice about the way I should go about looking, or what sort of thing I should look for?"

"I am an expert on the building," the colonel said sadly, "and I could talk about it for a year without repeating myself. But unfortunately, there is nothing I can say that would aid in your particular situation."

Joenes asked, "Do you think I will ever find the office I was sent to?"

"If your business here is important," the colonel said, "and if the high officials really want you to find the office, then I'm sure you'll have no trouble. On the other hand, your business may not be of importance to anyone but you, in which case your search will doubtless be a long one.

True, you carry official orders; but I suspect that the high officials occasionally send men to imaginary offices simply to test the security of the inner defences of the building. If that is the case with you, your chance of success is small indeed."

"One way or another," Joenes said gloomily, "my prospects don't look very good."

"Well, those are the risks all of us run here," the colonel said. "Spies suspect that their rulers have sent them on a dangerous mission simply to get rid of them, and mapmakers suspect that they are ordered to draw simply to keep their fingers out of mischief. We all have our doubts, and I can only wish you the best of luck and the hope that your doubts are never proved true."

With that, the colonel bowed courteously and walked down the corridor.

Joenes watched him go and considered following him. But he had already gone down that way, and it seemed a necessary act of faith to go forward into what he did not know rather than turn back at the first discouragement.

So Joenes went on, but not entirely out of faith. He also suspected that the corridors behind him might have been changed by now.

Joenes walked down great halls and corridors, up stairways, through bypasses, across lobbies, and down more corridors. He resisted the urge to consult his beautiful false map, but he couldn't bring himself to throw the thing away. So he kept it in his pocket and kept on walking.

There was no way to tell the passage of time, but at last Joenes became very weary. He was now in an ancient part of the building. The floors here were of wood rather than marble, and they were badly decayed, making the footing dangerous. The walls, built of an inferior plaster, were flaked and torn. In some places the plaster had fallen away to reveal the wiring of the building, most of its insulation rotten and constituting an obvious fire hazard. Not even the ceiling seemed secure; it bulged ominously in places, making Joenes fear it would come down on him.

Whatever offices had once been here were now gone, and the place was in need of immediate and drastic repairs. Joenes even saw a workman's hammer lying on the floor; this convinced him that repairs would be made someday, even though he didn't see any workmen.

Lost and deeply discouraged, Joenes lay down on the floor, his great fatigue allowing him no other choice. He stretched out and within a minute fell asleep.

### THE STORY OF THESEUS

Joenes awoke with a feeling of uneasiness. Standing up, he heard the sound of footsteps coming down the corridor.

Soon he saw the maker of the footsteps. He was a man, tall and in the prime of life, with a face both intelligent and suspicious. This man held a huge ball of string mounted on a spindle. As he walked, he unwound the string, which fell to the floor of the corridor and glittered faintly.

As soon as he saw Joenes, the man's face tightened into angry lines. He drew a revolver from his belt and took aim.

Joenes called out, "Wait! Whatever you think, I have never done you any harm! "

Controlling himself with obvious effort, the man did not pull the trigger. His eyes, which had gone blank and dangerous, regained a normal appearance. He put the revolver back in his belt and said, " I am very sorry to have startled you. The truth is, I thought you were someone else."

"Do I look like him? " Joenes asked.

"Not really," the man said. "But I become nervous in this damnable place and tend to shoot first and think second. Still, my mission is so vital that these actions of a hasty and high-strung nature can surely be forgiven."

"What is your mission?" Joenes asked.

The man's face glowed when Joenes asked that question. Proudly he said, "My mission is to bring peace, happiness, and freedom to the world."

"That's quite a lot," Joenes said.

"I could never be satisfied with anything less," the man said. "Mark my name well. It is George P. Theseus, and I confidently expect to be remembered as the man who destroyed dictatorship and freed the people. The deed I do here will live as a symbol to all men, and will also be good and just in its own right."

"What deed are you going to do" Joenes asked.

"Singlehanded, I am going to kill a tyrant," Theseus said. "This man has managed to find a position of power within the building, and many gullible fools think he is a benefactor because he orders the building of dams to control floods, distributes food to the starving, finances medical work for the sick, and does many other gaudy things of that sort. This may deceive some people, but it does not deceive me."

"If he really does that work," Joenes said, "then he does indeed sound like a benefactor."

"I might have expected you to say that," Theseus said bitterly. "His tricks have taken you in, just as they have taken in most people. I cannot hope to change your mind. I have no skill at devious argument, while that man has the world's best propagandists at his service. My vindication must rest with the future. For now, I can only tell what I know, and tell it in a blunt, unpleasing manner."

"I will be very pleased to hear," Joenes said.

"Well then," Theseus said, "consider this. In order to do

his good deeds, this man had to reach high office. To reach high office, he passed out bribes and sowed dissension, divided people into warring factions, killed off those who opposed him, corrupted the influential few, and starved the needy many. At last, when his power was absolute, he engaged in public works. But not out of love for the public. No, he did it as you or I might weed a garden, so that he might have something pleasant to look at instead of something ugly. This is how it is with tyrants, who will do anything to obtain power, and thereby create and perpetuate the very evils they purport to cure."

Joenes was moved by Theseus's speech, but a little suspicious also, because Theseus had a shifty and dangerous look. So Joenes spoke with caution: " I can certainly understand why you want to kill this man."

"No you can't," Theseus said morosely. "You probably think I'm filled with nothing but hot air and ideals, a sort of pious madman with a gun. Well, you're wrong. I'm an ordinary sort of man, and if I can perform a good deed and win a reputation, then I'm happy. But my action against this tyrant is primarily for personal reasons."

"How so? " Joenes asked.

"This tyrant," Theseus said, "has private tastes just as perverted as the wild passions that drove him to power. Information such as this is usually kept secret, or scoffed at as the ravings of envious fools. His skilled propagandists see to that. But I know the truth.

"This great man came driving through my town one day in his armoured black Cadillac, secure behind bulletproof glass, puffing a big cigar and waving to the crowds. Then his eye chanced to fall upon a little girl in the crowd, and he ordered his car to stop.

"His bodyguards chased the people away, except for a few who watched from cellars and rooftops, unseen but seeing. Then the tyrant stepped out of his car and walked up to the little girl. He offered her ice cream and sweets, and begged her to get into the car with him.

"Some of the watching men understood what was happening, and rushed out to rescue the child. But the bodyguards shot and killed those men. They did so with silenced guns so as not to startle the girl; they told her that the men had decided to go to sleep for a while.

"Although a complete innocent, the child had her suspicions. Something in the tyrant's sweating red face and thick trembling lips must have frightened her. So, even though she wanted the ice cream and candy, she stood irresolute while the tyrant trembled with lust, and those of us watching helplessly in the cellars sweated out of fear for her.

"After looking wistfully at the gorgeous array of sweets and observing the tyrant's nervous movements, the little girl made up her mind. She would go in the car, she said, if her playmates could go with her. In the terrible vulnerability of her innocence, the child thought she would be safe among her playmates.

"The tyrant went purple with joy. It was evident that this was more than he dared hope for. The more the merrier, that was his sinister motto. He told the girl to bring along all the playmates she wished, and the girl called for her friends.

"The children came flocking to the black Cadillac. They would have come even without her summons, for the tyrant had had the wit to turn on his car radio, which played the most marvellous and enticing music.

"Music playing, sweets distributed, the tyrant herded them all into his enormous car and shut the door. His bodyguard closed around him, mounted on their powerful motorcycles. Then they all sped away, bound for the most shameful debaucheries in the tyrant's private pleasure room. Those children have never been heard of again. And that first little girl, as you may have guessed, was my own sister, taken under my eyes, with townspeople lying dead on the pavement near her, and with me in the cellar powerless to help."

Theseus wiped his eyes, which were now streaming freely. He said to Joenes, "Now you know the real and personal reasons why I am going to kill the tyrant. To destroy his evil, to avenge my slain friends, to rescue the poor children, but above all, to find my poor sister. I am no hero, I am nothing but an ordinary man. But events have forced me to perform this righteous deed."

Joenes, whose own eyes were far from dry, embraced Theseus and said, "I wish you good fortune on your quest, and I certainly hope you can succeed against so terrible a tyrant."

"I have my hopes," Theseus said, "And I am not without the determination and guile necessary for this difficult work. To begin with, I sought out the tyrant's daughter. I ingratiated myself with her, used every winning way I could think of, until at last she fell in love with me. Then I debauched her, and this gave me some satisfaction since she was not far from my poor sister's age. She desired marriage, and I promised to marry her, although I would rather slit my throat. And I explained to her very artfully what sort of man her father was. At first she would not believe me, the little idiot loved her tyrant father so! But she loved me more, and slowly became convinced of the truth of everything I said. Then, as the final step, I sought her aid in my plan to kill her father. You can imagine how difficult that was. The horrible little girl did not want her daddy destroyed, no matter how evil he was, no matter what he had done. But I threatened to leave her for ever if she would not help me; and between love of me and love of her father she was nearly driven mad. Over and over she begged me to forget the past, which no action could erase.

147

Come away with her, she said, and live in some place far from her father, and never think of him but only of her. As though I could ever look at her and not see her father's features! For days she held back, thinking she could convince me to do what she wanted. Endlessly she declared her love for me, stating it in the most exaggerated and hysterical terms. She would never allow us to be parted, she swore, and if death should befall me, then she would kill herself, too. And a great deal of similar nonsense, which, as a sensible man, I found most distasteful.

"At last I turned from her and took my leave. Then her courage crumbled. This young monster, filled with the most exquisite self-loathing, said she would help me in murdering her beloved father, if only I would swear never to leave her. And of course I swore what she wanted. I would have promised anything to get the assistance I needed.

"She told me what she alone knew; where her father's office could be found in this great building. And she also gave me this ball of string so that I could mark my way and leave quickly once the deed was done. And she herself gave me this revolver. And so here I am, on my way to the tyrant's office."

Joenes said, "You have not found him yet, I see?"

"Not yet," Theseus answered. "The corridors here are very long and winding, as you must have observed yourself. Also, I've had some bad luck. As I mentioned, I am of a hasty disposition and therefore inclined to shoot first and think second. Because of that, quite accidentally, I shot and killed a man in officer's uniform not long ago. He came upon me suddenly, and I fired without thinking."

"Was it the mapmaker?" Joenes asked

"I do not know who he was," Theseus answered. "But he wore a colonel's badges, and he seemed to have a kindly face."

"It was the mapmaker," Joenes said.

"I am very sorry about it," Theseus said. "But I am even sorrier about the three others I killed in these hallways. I must be an unlucky man."

"Who were they?" Joenes asked.

"To my great sorrow, they were three of the children I had come to rescue. They must have slipped out of the tyrant's rooms and tried to reach freedom. I shot them as I shot the officer, and as I nearly shot you; that is, hastily, before they had a chance to speak. I cannot describe my feelings of regret, and my increased determination that the tyrant shall pay for all this."

"What will you do about his daughter?" Joenes asked

"I won't follow my natural instincts and kill her," Theseus said. "But that ugly little bitch will never see me again. And I will pray that the tyrant's whelp dies of a broken heart."

So saying, Theseus turned his wrathful countenance towards the dim corridor stretching before him.

"And now," he said, "I must go about my work. Goodbye, my friend, and wish me luck."

Theseus walked briskly away, unwinding his glittering cord as he went. Joenes watched until he had vanished around a corner. For a time he could hear receding footsteps, then there was no sound at all.

Suddenly a woman appeared in the corridor behind Joenes.

She was very young, hardly more than a child. She was plump and red-faced, and her eyes glittered insanely. She walked silently, following after Theseus. And as she walked, she gathered up the string he had so carefully laid down. She had a huge ball of it in her hands, and she continued winding as she came near Joenes, obliterating the trail by which Theseus had thought to return.

As she passed Joenes, she turned and looked at him, and her face was wild with rage and grief. She said not one word, but put a finger to her lips in the sign of silence. Then she walked swiftly on, gathering the string as she went.

She was gone as swiftly as she had come, and the corridor was deserted. Joenes stared in both directions, but saw nothing to indicate that either Theseus or the girl had ever passed his way. He rubbed his eyes, and once again lay down and fell asleep.

Some storytellers maintain that Joenes met with numerous other adventures while he was within the corridors of the Octagon. It is said that he encountered the Three Fates, and that those ancient crones explained to him their duties and desires, and from that Joenes grew to an understanding of the problems of the gods, and their ways of solving those problems. It is also said that Joenes slept on the floor of the corridor for twenty years, and that he awakened only through the intervention of Aphrodite Pandemos, who told him the story of her life. And when Joenes expressed disbelief at certain details of her story, the goddess changed our hero into a woman. In this form, Joenes underwent many difficulties and testings of the soul, to say nothing of the body, and learned many curious things that men, as a rule, never learn. And at last he acknowledged the truth of every detail of Aphrodite's story, and she changed him back into a man.

But there is only a limited authority for all this, and no details given. So now we will tell of Joenes's last adventure in the Octagon, which came as he lay asleep after his encounter with Theseus.

### THE STORY OF MINOTAURUS

Joenes was roughly shaken awake. He sprang to his feet, and saw that the hall around him was no longer ancient and decayed, but was now gleaming and modern. The man who had awakened him was very large through the shoulders, even larger in the paunch, and had a broad, stern, no-nonsense face. No one could have mistaken this man for anything but an official.

"You're Joenes?" the official asked. "Well, if you've finished your nap, I suppose we can get to work."

Joenes expressed his deep regret that he had been sleeping instead of looking for the office to which he had been sent.

"It doesn't matter," the official said. "We have our protocol here, but I hope we're not stuffy. As a matter of fact, it's just as well that you slept. I had been situated in an entirely different part of the building, and I received urgent orders from the Security Chief to move my office here and to effect any repairs I thought necessary. The workmen found you asleep and decided not to bother you. They did their work in silence, moving you only to repair the piece of floor you lay upon. You didn't even wake up when they moved you."

Joenes looked with increasing amazement at the vast amount of work that had been done while he slept. He turned to an office door, where before there had been only a decayed wall. On that door was neatly stencilied: Room 18891, Floor 12, Level 6, Wing 63, Subsection AJB-2. This was the exact address he had been looking for in vain; and Joenes expressed surprise at the manner in which his search had ended.

"Nothing to be surprised about," the official said. "This is quite an ordinary business procedure here. The highest officials not only know the building and all its contents, but they are also aware of every person's movements within the building. They know only too well the difficulties a stranger encounters here; and unfortunately, there are very strict laws against helping strangers. But the officials circumvent the law from time to time by moving the office to meet the searcher. Reasonable, eh? Now come in and we'll get to work."

Within the office there was a large desk piled high with papers, and three ringing telephones. The official asked Joenes to take a chair while he dealt with the telephones. He did so with the utmost dispatch.

"Speak up man!" he roared into the first telephone. "What's that? Mississippi flooding again? Build a dam! Build ten dams, but get it under control. Send me a memo when you're finished.

"Yes, I can hear you," he shouted into the second telephone. "Starvation in the Panhandle? Distribute food at once! Just sign my name at the government warehouse.

"Calm down and let's hear about it," he bellowed into the third telephone. "Plague sweeping Los Angeles? Get vaccine in there at once, and send me a wire when it's under control."

The official put down the last of his telephones and said to Joenes. "These idiotic assistants of mine panic at the slightest thing. And as if that weren't bad enough, those gutless wonders wouldn't pull a drowning baby out of a bathtub without calling me first for authorization!"

Joenes had listened to the official's swift and decisive words over the telephones, and a suspicion had crossed his mind. He said, "I'm not absolutely certain of this, but I believe that a certain aggrieved young man——"

"—is trying to assassinate me," the official finished for him. "That's it, isn't it? Well, I took care of him half an hour ago. You don't catch Edwin J. Minotaurus napping. My guards took him away, and he'll probably get life imprisonment. But don't tell anyone."

"Why not?" Joenes asked.

"Bad publicity," Minotaurus said. "Especially his affair with my daughter, whom, incidentally, he knocked up,

152

I've told that little half-wit to bring her friends to the house, but no, she has to sneak out and have dates with anarchists! We're giving out a specially prepared story that this Theseus fellow wounded me so severely that the doctors have despaired of my life; and that he escaped and married my daughter. You can see the value of a story like that."

"Not too clearly," Joenes said.

"Why damn it all, it builds up sympathy for me!" Minotaurus said. "People will feel sorry when they hear I'm at the point of death. And they'll feel even sorrier when they learn that my only daughter has married my assassin. You see, in spite of my proven abilities, the rabble doesn't like me. This story should win them over."

"It's very ingenious," Joenes said.

"Thank you," said Minotaurus. "Frankly, I had been worrying about my public image for quite some time, and if this moron with his string and his revolver hadn't come along, I would have had to hire somebody. I just hope the newspapers handle the story properly."

"Is there any doubt about that?" Joenes said.

"Oh, they'll print what I tell them," Minotaurus said moodily. "And I've hired a man to do a book about it, and there'll be a play and a movie based on the book. Don't worry, I'll milk this for all it's worth."

"What have you told them to write about your daughter?" Joenes asked.

"Well, as I said, she marries this anarchist fellow. And then in a year or two we publish an account of their divorce. Have to give the child a name, you know. But God knows what those idiots will write about my poor fat little Ariadne. Probably make her out to be beautiful, thinking it will please me. And the filthy scum who read this sort of thing will cry, and ask for more. Even kings and presidents, who should know better, will read these lies in preference to a good honest book of statistics. The human race is largely composed of incompetent, lying, bungling fools. I can control them, but I'll be damned if I can understand them."

"What about the children?" Joenes asked.

"What do you mean, what about the children?" Minotaurus said, glaring fiercely.

"Well, Theseus said——"

"That man is a gifted but insane liar," Minotaurus stated. "If it weren't for my position, I'd have sued him for libel. Children! Do I look like some kind of pervert? I think we can safely forget any question of children. Now, shall we get down to you and your work?"

Joenes nodded, and Minotaurus gave him a quick briefing on the political situation he was likely to find in Russia. He showed Joenes a secret map that gave the approximate positions and strengths of Communist and Western forces all over the earth. Joenes was stunned by the hugeness of the enemy forces, painted blood-red and stretching across many countries. The Western forces, painted sky-blue, seemed entirely inadequate.

"It isn't as hopeless as it looks," Minotaurus said. "For one thing, that map is only guesswork. For another, we do possess an enormous stockpile of warheads, and a missile system to carry them. We've come a long way with our missiles. The real proof came last year during the Combat Team Easy field exercises. At that time, a single Gnome missile with an improved warhead was able to blow up Io, one of the moons of Jupiter where we had simulated a Russian base."

"That certainly sounds as though we have strength," Joenes said.

"Oh yes. But the Russians and Chinese also have improved missiles, which succeeded four years ago in blowing up the planet Neptune. In effect, that means a missile stalemate. There may be some disaffection between the Russians and the Chinese because of the Yingdraw incident; but we can't count on that."

"What can we count on?" Joenes asked

"Nobody knows," Minotaurus said. "That's why we're sending you on find out. *Information* is our problem, Joenes. What is the enemy actually up to? What in hell is going on over there? I know that John Mudge of Services Co-ordination told you of our need for the truth, no matter how terrible, told bluntly and forthrightly by a man we can trust. Do you understand the task we are setting you, Joenes?"

"I think I do," Joenes said.

"You are to serve no group or faction; and above all you are not to make the sort of report you think we would *like* to hear. You are neither to minimize nor to maximize the things you see, but to state them as simply and as objectively as possible."

"I will do my best," Joenes said.

"I don't suppose I can ask for more," Minotaurus said grudgingly.

Then Minotaurus gave Joenes the money and papers he would need for his trip. And instead of sending him back into the corridors to find his way to the entrance, Minotaurus opened a window and pressed a button.

"This is the way I always do it," Minotaurus said, helping Joenes into the seat beside the pilot. "Can't be bothered with all those damned corridors. Good luck, Joenes, and remember what I've said."

Joenes said that he would. He felt deeply touched by the faith Minotaurus had in him. The helicopter moved away towards the Washington Airport, where a special autopilot jet would be waiting. But as the helicopter rose, Joenes thought he heard children's laughter from a room adjoining Minotaurus' office.

## 12. THE STORY OF RUSSIA

*(As told by Pelui of Easter Island)*

JOENES boarded his special jet, and soon he was high in the air racing northward towards the pole. A meal was served to him automatically, and later a movie was shown for his solitary pleasure. The sun hung low on the horizon, and at last the jet's automatic pilot asked Joenes to fasten his seat belt for the landing at Moscow Airport.

The landing was made without incident; and Joenes waited with mingled feelings of excitement and apprehension as the door of the jet swung open upon the capital of the Communist world.

Joenes was met by three officials of the Soviet government. They were clad in fur hats and coats, and fur-lined boots, necessary protection against the freezing wind that howled across the flat fields. They introduced themselves and took Joenes to a waiting command car for the drive into Moscow. During this ride, Joenes had a chance to look more closely at the men he was to deal with.

Comrade Slavski was bearded to his eyes, which had a dreamy, faraway look in their hazel depths.

Comrade Oruthi was small and clean-shaven, and he walked with a limp.

Marshal Trigask was round and cheerful, and seemed a man to be reckoned with.

At Red Square they parked in front of the Peace Hall. Within, a cheerful fire was blazing. The Russians gestured Joenes to a comfortable chair, and took seats beside him.

"We shall waste no words," Marshal Trigask said. "I

shall merely preface this discussion by welcoming you to our beloved Moscow. We are always pleased when accredited Western diplomats such as yourself come to visit us. We are plain speakers, and we expect plain speaking in return. That is how to get things done. You may have noticed on your drive into Moscow——"

"Yes," broke in Slavski, "you must excuse me, I beg your pardon, but did you notice the little white snow crystals falling? And the white winter sky? I'm really very sorry, I shouldn't speak, but even a man such as myself has feelings and sometimes feels impelled to express them. Nature, gentlemen! Excuse me, but nature, yes, there is something about it. . . ."

Marshal Trigask interrupted: "This is enough, Slavski. The most excellent Presidential Envoy Joenes has, I am sure, noticed nature at some time or another. I think we can dispense with such niceties. I am a plain man and I want to speak plainly. Perhaps I seem crude to you, but there it is. I am a soldier, and I cannot be bothered with diplomat's manners. Have I made myself clear?"

"Yes, quite clear," Joenes said.

"Excellent," Marshal Trigask went on. "In that case, what is your answer?"

"My answer to what?" Joenes asked.

"To our latest proposals," Trigask said. "Surely you haven't come all this long way simply for a vacation?"

"I'm afraid you'll have to tell me about your proposals," Joenes said.

"They're really very simple," Comrade Oruthi said. "We merely ask that your government dismantle its arms, give up its colony of Hawaii, allow us to take possession of Alaska (which was originally ours), and also give us the northern half of California as a sign of good faith. Upon those terms we will undertake to do various things that I have forgotten at the moment. What do you say?"

Joenes tried to explain that he had no authority to say anything, but the Russians were unwilling to accept that. Therefore, knowing that such terms would never be accepted in Washington, he said no.

"You see?" Oruthi said. "I told you they'd say no."

"It was worth a try, wasn't it?" Marshal Trigask said. "After all, they might have said yes. But now we can get down to fundamentals. Mr. Joenes, I want you and your government to know that we are prepared to repel any attack of any size that you may mount against us."

"Our defences begin in Eastern Germany," Oruthi said, "and they run in breadth from the Baltic to the Mediterranean."

"In depth," Marshal Trigask said, "they extend completely through Germany and Poland, and through most of European Russia. You may inspect those defences and see for yourself our states of preparedness. Furthermore, our defences are fully automatic, more modern than those of Western Europe, and more densely situated. In short, we are still ahead of you. We have outdefended you, and will be happy to prove it."

Slavski, who had been silent for a long time, now said, "You will see all this, my friend! You will see the starlight glittering on the gun barrels! I beg your pardon, but even a humble man like me, a man who might be mistaken for a fishmonger or a carpenter, has his poetic moments. Yes, it is true even though you laugh, gentlemen! Did not our poet say: 'Dark is the grass/ When night shall creep/ Away in sorrow.' Ah, you had not thought to hear me quote poetry! Let me assure you, I am quite aware of the impropriety of my quoting poetry! I regret my conduct more than you could imagine, I deplore it in fact, and yet . . ."

Comrade Oruthi gently joggled Slavski's shoulder, and he fell silent. Oruthi said, "You must forget his outbursts, Mr.

Joenes. He is a leading Party theoretician, and therefore has a tendency towards self-conscious speech. Where are we?"

"I think I had just explained," Marshal Trigask said, "that our defences are completely in order.'

"Exactly," Oruthi said. "Your government should not be deceived in that account. Nor should they attach any importance to the Yingdraw incident. Your propagandists have doubtless represented that in many false ways. But the truth is quite simple, and came about through a simple misunderstanding."

"I was there at the time," Marshal Trigask said, "and can tell you exactly what happened. My command, the People's First, Eighth, Fifteenth, and Twenty-fifth Armies, were holding field exercises at Yingdraw near the border of the Chinese People's Republic. During these exercises we were murderously attacked by a revisionist band of turncoat Chinese who had been subverted by Western gold, and who had somehow eluded the Peiping authorities."

"I was political commissar at the time," Oruthi said, "and I can attest the truth of what the Marshal is saying. These bandits came at us under the guise of the Chinese People's Fourth, Twelfth, Thirteenth, and Thirty-second Armies. Naturally we informed Peiping, and then took steps to drive the turncoats over the border."

"They, of course, insisted that they were driving *us* back over the border," Marshal Trigask said, with an ironic smile. "This was what we expected rebels to say, so battle was joined. In the meantime, we had received a message from Peiping. Unfortunately, it was written in ideograms. We were unable to read it, and sent it to Moscow for translation. In the meantime battle raged, and for a week both sides blazed away at each other."

"The translation came back," Oruthi said. "It read: 'The government of the Chinese People's Republic resents

159

any implication of expansionism on its part, especially in regard to the rich, empty lands adjacent to the crowded Chinese borders. There are no rebels within the territorial limits of the Chinese People's Republic, and none are possible in a truly socialistic state. Therefore cease your warlike attacks upon our peaceful frontiers.'"

"You can imagine our perplexity," Marshal Trigask said. "The Chinese insisted that there were no rebels, and we were fighting at least a million of them, all of whom had stolen uniforms from the Chinese People's Army."

"Luckily," Oruthi said, "a high Kremlin official had come to advise us. This man was an expert on China. He told us we could ignore the first part of the message about expansionism, since this was meant in the form of a salutation. The second part about the non-existence of rebels, was obviously designed to save face. Accordingly he advised us to push the rebels back into China."

"That, however, was quite difficult," Marshal Trigask said. "The rebels had been reinforced by several million armed men, and by sheer weight of numbers had pushed us back all the way to Omsk, sacking Semipalatinsk on their way."

"Seeing that the situation showed signs of seriousness," Oruthi said, "we called in reserves. These came to no less than twenty Russian armies. With these we gloriously slaughtered an uncountable number of rebels, and pushed the rest back completely across Sinkiang into Szechuan."

"We thought that took care of the matter," Marshal Trigask said. "We were marching to Peking to exchange views with the Chinese People's Government when the rebels suddenly renewed the attack. Their force now numbered some fifty million men. Luckily, not all of these were armed."

"Even the gold of the West has its limits," Oruthi said.

"We received another note from Peiping," Marshal

Trigask said. "In translation, this one told us to leave the territory of China immediately, and to cease our warlike assaults against the defensive elements of the Chinese People's Army."

"We think that's what the note meant," Oruthi said. "But with fiendish cleverness, they had constructed their message so that, when read upside down, it became a poem which went: 'How beautiful is the mountain/ floating in the river/ past my garden.'"

"Most ironic," Marshal Trigask said, "was the fact that, by the time we deciphered their message, we had been pushed back many thousands of miles from the borders of China, all the way across high Asia to Stalingrad. There we made a stand, slaughtered millions, and were thrown back again to Kharkov, where we made a stand, and were once more thrown back to Kiev. Again we were forced back, making another stand outside of Warsaw. By this time we considered the situation to be serious. We gathered together volunteer armies from Eastern Germany, Poland, Czechoslovakia, Rumania, Hungary, and Bulgaria. The Albanians treacherously joined the Greeks who, with the Yugoslavs, attacked us from the rear. We threw off the attack and concentrated our forces for the main effort to the east. This time we attacked the Chinese rebels with our full armies and reserves, along a seven-hundred-mile front. We rolled the rebel forces back the entire way they had come, and farther, all the way to Canton, which we devastated."

"There," Oruthi continued, "the rebels threw in their last few million reserves, and we fell back to the border. After regrouping, we fought a series of border engagements for several months. At last, by mutual consent, we both withdrew."

"I still wanted to press the attack," Marshal Trigask said. "But more cautious leaders pointed out that I had only a few thousand ragged men left with which to oppose the decimated but still determined rebels. This would not have stopped me; but my colleague Oruthi pointed out, most correctly, that it was now a purely internal matter for the Chinese. That ended the Yingdraw incident."

"We have been unable to contact Peking since that time," Oruthi said. "But the pique of our great ally will pass."

"I must add only," Trigask said, "that no one in the West knows the full extent of this incident, since neither we nor the Chinese told about it, and the few informers who did were not believed. You might, I suppose, wonder why we tell you the story in such detail?"

"I was wondering that," Joenes said.

"We tell it because we know where your true sympathies lie, *Comrade Jonski*."

"I beg your pardon?" Joenes said.

"Oh, we know," Oruthi said. "We have our ways of finding things out. Not even the darkest machinations of the American Congress can be hidden from us. We know of the Communist speech you made in San Francisco, and of your subsequent inquisition by a congressional committee. We saw how the American secret police followed you, since we followed them. And of course, the associates of Arnold and Ronald Black told us of the great services you had done for the cause, and of the cleverness with which you avoided all contacts with them. Finally, we observed how successful you were in re-establishing yourself in the government's favour and in acquiring a key position. Therefore we say, welcome home, comrade!"

"I am not a comrade," Joenes answered. "And I am serving the American cause to the best of my ability."

"Well said," Trigask said. "Who knows who may be listening, eh? You did right in keeping your cover, and I for one shall not bring the matter up again. We want you to keep that cover, *Mister* Joenes, because in that way you are most valuable to us."

"Correct," Oruthi said. "The matter is closed. You will use your own judgment, *Mister* Joenes, as to what portion of the events of Yingdraw to tell. Word of apparent dissension with our allies might make your government more eager to negotiate, eh?"

"Remember to tell them," Trigask said, "that our missile arm is fully prepared, even though our conventional infantry forces may be somewhat reduced. We also have fully armed missile forces on the moon, Mars, and Venus. They are ready to rain down destruction whenever we give the word."

"Of course, giving the word is a little difficult," Oruthi said. "Speaking only among ourselves, there are certain adverse conditions that our spacemen have found. On the moon, they live deep underground in order to avoid solar radiation, and are continually occupied in trying to manufacture food, water, and air. This state of affairs renders communication difficult."

"On Venus," Slavski said, "the climate is so unbelievably humid that metal rusts with extreme rapidity, and plastic or vegetable products rot under one's very nose. This is hard on radio equipment."

"On Mars," Trigask said, "there are tiny, wormlike creatures of great malevolence. Although mindless, they eat their way into anything, even solid metal. Without unusual precautions, all of the equipment, to say nothing of the men themselves, can become honeycombed with these horrible creatures."

"I'm glad the Americans face the same problems," Oruthi said. "They also have sent expeditionary forces to the moon, Mars, and Venus. But we got there first, and therefore the planets belong to us. But now, Joenes, we really must offer you some refreshment."

Joenes was fed great quantities of yoghurt and black bread, which was all that was available at the moment. Then they went with Joenes in his own jet to show him the fortifications.

Soon Joenes could look down and see row upon row of cannon, minefields, barbed wire, machine guns, and pill-boxes, extending endlessly to the horizon, disguised as farms, villages, towns, troikas, droshkys, and the like. Joenes saw no people, however, and this reminded him of what he had heard earlier about the state of affairs in Western Europe.

They returned to Moscow Airport and the Russians disembarked, wishing Joenes good fortune on his return to Washington.

Just before he left, Comrade Slavski said to him, "Remember, my friend, that all men are brothers. Oh, you may laugh at such fine sentiments coming from a drunkard who cannot even be counted on to do his work properly. Nor would I blame you for laughing, no more than I blamed my chief, Rosskolenko, for clubbing me over the ear yesterday and saying that I would lose my job if I showed up drunk again. I do not blame Rosskolenko, I love that terrible man as a brother, even though I know that I will get drunk again, and that he will fire me. And what will happen then to my eldest daughter, Grustikaya, who patiently mends my shirt and does not curse me when I steal her savings for drink? I can see that you despise me, and I do not blame you. No man could be more despicable than I. You may abuse me, gentlemen, and yet I am an educated man, I have noble sentiments, a great future once lay before me. . . ."

At this point Joenes's jet took off, and Joenes was unable to hear the end of Slavski's speech, if that speech had an end.

It was only later that Joenes reviewed all he had seen

and heard, and realized that there was no need for a war, nor even an excuse for fighting under present circumstances. The forces of chaos had overwhelmed the Soviets and Chinese, just as it had the West Europeans. But there was no reason now for that to happen in America.

This message, with full details, Joenes sent ahead of him to Washington.

# 13. THE STORY OF THE WAR

*(As told by Teleu of Huahine)*

IT is sad to relate that as Joenes flew over California an automatic radar station identified his jet as an invader, and fired a number of air-to-air missiles at it. This tragic incident marked the opening phase of the great war.

Mistakes of this kind have occurred throughout the history of warfare. But in twenty-first-century America, due to the great confidence and affection men had for their machines, and due also to the semi-autonomous nature of those machines, such a mistake was bound to have dire consequences.

Joenes watched with horror and fascination as the missiles speeded towards his jet. Then he felt a violent lurch as the jet's automatic pilot, sensing the danger, fired its own anti-missile-missiles in defence.

This attack brought other ground-based missile stations to the attack. Some of these stations were automatic and others were not, but all responded instantly to the emergency call. Joenes's jet, in the meantime, had expended its entire armament.

But it had not lost the guile its planners had built into it. It switched its radio to the missile-dispatching frequency and broadcast an alarm, declaring itself under attack and naming the airborne missiles as enemy targets to be destroyed.

These tactics met with some success. A number of the older, more simple-minded missiles would not destroy a craft they considered their own. The newer, more sophisticated missiles, however, had been alerted to just such an attempt on the part of an enemy. Therefore they pressed the attack, while the older missiles fiercely defended the solitary jet.

When the battle between the missiles was fully under way, Joenes's jet glided away from the area. With the battle zone far behind, the jet streaked for its home airport in Washington, D.C.

Upon arrival, Joenes was taken by elevator to the Service Command Post, seven hundred feet underground. Here he was questioned as to the nature of the assault upon him and the identity of the assailants. But all Joenes could say for certain was that he had been attacked by some missiles and defended by others.

This was already known, so the officers questioned the automatic pilot of Joenes's jet.

For a time the automatic pilot gave evasive answers, since the proper security code had not been read to it. But after this was done, it stated that ground-based missiles had attacked it over California, and that some of these missiles were of a type it had never seen before.

This and all other data concerning the battle were given to the War Probabilities Calculator, which quickly presented the following choices in order of apparent probability:

1. The Communist Bloc had attacked California.
2. The neutralist countries had attacked California.
3. The members of the Western Alliance had attacked California.
4. Invaders from outer space had attacked California.
5. There was no attack upon California.

The calculator also gave all possible combinations and permutations of these five possibilities, and ranked them as alternate sub-possibilities.

Joenes's earlier report on the state of affairs in Russia and China had also been received in Washington, but had not yet been processed and approved by the slow and methodical Human Factors and Reliability Assessment Calculator. This was a shame, since the War Probabilities Calculator could use only material that had been verified by other calculators.

The attending officers found themselves bewildered by the many probabilities, sub-probabilities, possibilities and sub-possibilities they were given. They had hoped to choose the statement rated most probable, and to act upon it. But the War Probabilities Calculator rendered that impossible. As new data came in, the calculator revised and refined its probabilities, ranking and grouping them in ever-changing sequences. Reappraisal sheets marked MOST URGENT spewed from the machine at the rate of ten a second, no two alike, to the annoyance of the attending officers.

Still, the machine was only doing what an ideal intelligence officer would have done—taking into account all approved reports, weighing their meaning and their probability, making recommendations on the basis of all pertinent and verifiable information, and never holding to an opinion out of mere pride or stubbornness, but remaining always ready and willing to revise any judgment on the basis of new data.

To be sure, the War Probabilities Calculator issued no orders; the issuing of orders was the glory and responsibility of men. Nor could the calculator be blamed for not presenting a unified, true, and consistent picture of the hostilities over California; it was impossible to give such a picture. The very nature of warfare in the twenty-first century had created this impossibility.

No longer did a commander march at the head of his army and see before him the men of an opposing army, standing behind their own general, dressed in their own particular colours, flying battle flags, singing martial airs—all these things giving unmistakable sensory proof as to the existence, nature, and identity of the enemy. Those days were past, and warfare had moved in step with industrial civilization, becoming more complex and more mechanical, and receding further from the men who were in command. Over the years, the generals were forced to stay at greater and greater distances from the actual clash of arms, in order to maintain a sure communication with all the interlocking men and machines that a battle utilized.

This had reached its epitome in Joenes's time. So it is no wonder that the officers took the Calculator's first five major possibilities, rated them equally, and brought them to General Voig, Commander of the Armed Forces, for him to render final decision.

Voig, studying the five alternatives before him, was aware of the problems of modern warfare, and sadly recognized how dependent he was on information upon which to base a sound decision. He also knew that most of his information came to him from extremely expensive machines that sometimes could not tell the difference between a goose and a rocket; machines that required regiments of highly trained men to minister to them, repair them, improve them, and to soothe them in every way. And even with all this lavish attention, Voig knew that the machines could not really be trusted. The creations were no better than the creators, and indeed resembled them in many of the worst ways. Like men, the machines were frequently subject to something resembling emotional instability. Some became overzealous, others had recurring hallucinations, functional and psychosomatic breakdowns, or even complete catatonic withdrawals. And aside from their own problems, the machines tended to be influenced by the emotional states of their human operators. In fact, the more suggestible machines were nothing more than extensions of their operators' personalities.

General Voig knew, of course, that no machine possessed a real consciousness, and therefore no machine really suffered from the diseases of consciousness. But they *seemed* to, and that was just as bad as the real thing.

Men of the early industrial age had always assumed that machines would be cold, efficient, uncaring, and invariably correct. These romantics had been wrong, and General Voig knew that machines, despite their special senses and abilities, could not be trusted any more than men. So he sat and studied the five alternatives, thousands of miles from the battle, while dubious machines sent in their information, and hysterical men confirmed it.

In spite of the problems, General Voig was a man who had been trained to make decisions. And now, after a last look at the five alternatives, and a rapid questioning of his own knowledge and opinions, Voig picked up a telephone and issued his orders.

We do not know which of the five alternatives the General chose, or what his orders were. It made no difference. The battle had moved entirely out of the General's hands, and he was powerless to press the attack or to order it stopped, or to have any important effect upon the hostilities. The fight had become uncontrollable, and this condition had been hastened because of the semi-autonomous nature of the machines.

A wounded California missile screamed high into the heavens and crashed at Cape Canaveral in Florida, destroying half the base. The remaining half rallied and launched retaliatory missiles at an enemy apparently entrenched in California. Other missiles, damaged but not destroyed, crashed in all parts of the country. Local commanders in New York, New Jersey, Pennsylvania, and many other states, struck back on their own authority, as did the automatic missile stations. Both men and machines had no lack of intelligence reports upon which to base this decision. In fact, before their communications were disrupted, they had received a deluge of reports covering every possibility. Being soldiers, they chose the most dire.

Throughout California and all of Western America, this retaliation was retaliated against. Local commanders believed that the enemy, whoever he was, had established beachheads on America's east coast. They sought to destroy these beachheads, not hesitating to use atomic warheads when they deemed it necessary.

All of this took place with a terrible rapidity. The local commanders and their machines, subjected to a hellish rain of fire, tended to fight back as long as they could. Some may have waited for specific orders; but in the end all fought who could fight, compounding destruction and confusion, and spreading it to all corners of the world. And soon the civilization of proliferating machinery had vanished from the face of the earth.

While this was taking place, Joenes stood bewildered in the Services Command Post, watching generals give orders and other generals countermand them. All of this Joenes saw, and still could not say of his own knowledge who or what the enemy was.

At this point the Command Post gave a vast shudder. Although situated many hundreds of feet underground, it had now come under attack by special burrowing machines.

Joenes flung out a hand to keep his balance, and grasped the shoulder of a young first lieutenant. The lieutenant turned, and Joenes recognized him at once

"Lum!" he cried.

"Hey, Joenesy!" Lum said in reply.

"How did you get here?" Joenes asked. "And what are you doing in the Army as a lieutenant?"

"Well, man," Lum said, "that is quite a tale, and it is all the more strange because I am not exactly what one would have called the military sort. But I am very glad you asked me that question."

The Command Post shuddered once again, throwing many officers to the floor. But Lum contrived to keep his balance, and he told Joenes the story of how he had joined the Army.

## 14. HOW LUM JOINED THE ARMY

*(Lum's own words, as recorded in the* Book of Fiji, *Orthodox Edition)*

WELL, man, I left the Hollis Home for the Criminally Insane shortly after you, and I went to New York and attended a really swinging party. It so happened I got high on C that night, which is nasty stuff if you aren't used to it, which I was not. I mean I've always been a peyote man, and heroin never interested me, and I thought that cocaine was merely one of those old-fashioned kicks until I tried it that night.

But I did try it, and I got this feeling whilst with the big C that I had a Florence Nightingale type duty to tend all the sick fighting machines of the world. The more I thought about it the surer I was, and the sadder I became as I thought of poor suffering old machine guns with burned-out barrels, tanks with rust in their treads, jets with broken landing gears, and the like. I thought of the terrible dumb agony these machines go through, and I knew that I had to heal and comfort them.

As you can see, I was pretty well gassed, and in that state I marched down to the nearest recruiting station and joined up so as to be close to the poor machines.

The next day I woke up and found myself in the Army, and it was a sobering not to say a frightening thought. I rushed out to find that damned enlistment sergeant who had taken advantage of a poor hophead obviously not in his right mind at the time, but he had flown to a Chicago whorehouse to give an enlistment speech. So I hastened to see my commanding officer, also called the CO, and told him that among other things I was a dope addict and a recent inmate of an institution for the criminally insane, both of which I could prove. And that furthermore I had latent homosexual tendencies, an overpowering fear of fire-arms, one blind eye, and also a bad back. Because of all this, I said, I could not legally be accepted into the armed services because of the provisions on page 123 paragraph C of the Enlistment Act.

The CO looked me straight in the eye and smiled in that way only a Regular Army man or a cop can smile. He said, "Soldier, this is the first day of your new life, so I am going to overlook certain irregularities in your manner of address-ing me. Now kindly get the hell out of here and report to the sergeant for duty."

When I didn't go, he stopped smiling and said, "Look, soldier, nobody cares about your reasons for enlisting, or for your so-called dope jag at the time. As for the various debilities you mentioned, don't worry about them. Hop-heads have done a first-class job in Planning, and nobody can laugh at the exploits of the Homosexual Brigade dur-ing the last police action in Patagonia. All you have to do is be a good soldier and you'll find that the Army is a good way of life. And do not go round quoting the Enlistment Act like a guardhouse lawyer, because that will make you unpopular with my sergeants, who just might beat your head to a pulp. Right? Right. Now we know where we stand, and I bear you no hard feelings. In fact I congratulate you on the patriotic zeal which led you to sign up for the special fifty-year full-duty enlistment last night. Good man! Now get the hell out of here."

So I left his office and wondered what to do next, since you can get out of a jail or an asylum, but not out of the Army. I was pretty down for a while, but then suddenly I was given a commission as a second lieutenant, and directly after that I was assigned to the personal staff of General Voig, who is the very topmost of the top brass.

At first I thought all this had happened because of my pleasing personality, but then I found out it was something else entirely. It appears that when enlisting, sky-high on coke, I had put down my occupation as pimp. This came to the attention of officers who watch for special occupational groups. In my case it was reported to General Voig, who immediately put in an order for me and my services.

At first I had no idea what to do, since I had never worked in that field. But another general's pimp, or Special Duty Officer, as he is more politely called, gave me the word. I thenceforth arranged a party for General Voig every Thursday night, this being the only night he could spare from his military duties. It is easy work, since all I need do is put in a call to one of the numbers listed in the Washington Defence Area Recreation Book; or, in a pinch, I send a hurry message to the Armed Services Procurement Department, which has branches in all major cities. The General has shown a hearty approval of my efficient work, and I must confess that the Army is not the grim and terrible place I had imagined it to be.

And that, Joenes, is what brings me here. Speaking as General Voig's aide and good friend, I can tell you that this war, whoever in hell we're fighting, could not be in better hands. I think this is important for all men to know, since lies are frequently told about men in high positions.

Furthermore, Joenesy, I think I should point out that there has just been an explosion here in the Command Post, and this hints of greater things to come. Also a few lights have gone off, and the air is growing just a shade musty. Therefore, since our services are obviously not needed down here, I suggest that you and I split this scene and cut out entirely, if such indeed is still possible.

Are you with me, Joenesy? Are you all right man?

# 15. THE ESCAPE FROM AMERICA

*(As told by Paaui of Fiji)*

JOENES had been stunned by a small explosion occurring near his head. In a state of shock, he let his friend lead him to an elevator that plunged them still deeper into the bowels of the earth. When they opened the elevator door, they were standing in a wide passageway. Ahead of them was a sign, reading: EMERGENCY UNDERGROUND SURVIVAL ROADWAY, FOR AUTHORIZED PERSONNEL ONLY.

Lum said, "I don't know if we are authorized personnel, but technicalities must be forgotten at a time like this. Joenes, are you able to speak? Straight ahead should be a vehicle that will carry us to what I sure as hell hope is safety. The General told me about this set-up, and I trust the old buzzard wasn't merely having his bit of fun."

They found the vehicle where Lum had expected it to be, and drove underground for many hours until they emerged on the eastern shore of Maryland, facing the Atlantic Ocean.

Here Lum's vigorous will faltered, and he was unable to think what to do next. But Joenes had recovered full possession of his senses. Taking Lum by the arm, he went down to the silent beach. Then he turned south and walked for several hours, coming at last to a deserted little harbour.

Joenes selected one sailing ship from the many that lay at the docks, and began transferring to it food, water, charts, and nautical instruments, taking them from the many other sea-going ships in the harbour. The job was not half done when missiles began screaming overhead, and Joenes decided to cast off immediately.

The boat was several miles out to sea before Lum roused himself, looked around, and asked, "Uh, man, like where we bound?"

"To my home," Joenes said. "To the island of Manituatua in the South Pacific."

Lum considered that, and said mildly, "Sort of a long trip, isn't it? I mean, what with rounding Cape Horn and all that jazz, it's probably something like eight or nine thousand miles, huh?"

"Something like that," Joenes said.

"You wouldn't maybe consider going to Europe instead, which is only like three thousand miles?"

"I'm going home," Joenes said firmly.

"Yeah. Well," Lum said, "east or west, home's the best. But we're somewhat short of food and water for a trip like this, and I suspect that little may be available along the way. Nor do I have the most perfect confidence in this boat, which I believe is already beginning to leak."

"All quite true," Joenes said. "But I think the leaks can be fixed. As for food and water, we'll hope for the best. Lum, there's really no other place that I know of worth going to."

"O.K.," Lum said. "I wasn't knocking it, I just thought I'd kick around a few thoughts to see if they would roll away. Since they won't, I, like you, will simply hope for the best. Also I think you should write your memoirs during this jaunt, since they would make interesting reading, and would serve to identify our poor starved cadavers should someone happen to come across this boat."

"I am not at all convinced that we are going to die," Joenes said, "though I must admit it seems a strong possibility. But why don't you write yours, Lum?"

"I may write a sketch or two," Lum said. "But for the

177

most part I am going to think about men and governments and how to improve them, bringing to the task every resource of my hophead mind."

"I think that's admirable, Lum," Joenes said. "Together we have many things to tell people, if only we can find people to tell things to."

Thus, in perfect accord, Joenes and his loyal friend set sail upon a darkening sea, down a perilous coast, towards a distant and uncertain goal.

# 16.  THE END OF THE JOURNEY

*(Written by the Editor and compiled from all available sources)*

OF their voyage down the coasts of the two Americas, around Cape Horn, and then northwest to the islands of the South Pacific, very little need be said. The trials that Joenes and Lum underwent were severe, and the dangers they faced were many. But this has been true in equal degree for a multitude of sailors throughout all ages, including our own. We note with profound pity how Joenes and Lum suffered under the tropical sun, were tossed by hurricanes, ran short of food and water, had their craft damaged, lost a mast, saw dangerous reefs to leeward, and so forth. But having expressed our sympathy, we must also observe that the details are the same as those told in countless other tales of small-boat passages. This sameness does not detract from the value of the experience; but it does cause a certain slackening of interest on the part of the reader.

Joenes himself never spoke to any great extent about that terrible trip, since he was interested in other things. And the only words Lum is reported to have said, when asked about his sensations during the voyage, were, " Well, man, you know."

We do indeed know. So we pass on to Joenes and Lum at their journey's end, starved but still living, unconscious and cast up on the shore, and nursed back to health by the inhabitants of Manituatua.

When he recovered his senses, Joenes inquired about his sweetheart Tondelayo, whom he had left in the islands.

But that high-spirited girl had grown tired of waiting, had married a fisherman from the Tuamotos, and was now the mother of two children. Joenes accepted this with good grace, and turned his attention to world affairs

He found that only a few effects of the war had been noted on Manituatua and its neighbouring islands. These islands, long out of touch with Asia and Europe, had suddenly lost communication with America. Wild rumours poured in. Some said there had been a great war in which all the great countries of the earth had destroyed each other. Others put the blame on alien invaders of an unbelievably malevolent disposition. Some said there had been no war at all, but rather a plague, followed by a general collapse of Western civilization.

These and many other theories were argued, and are argued still. Your editor holds to the view expressed by Joenes, of a spontaneous and chaotic explosion of warfare, culminating in the destruction of America, the last of the great civilizations of the Old World.

Little effect of this could be noticed on the islands of the South Pacific. Rumours were rampant, and missiles were sometimes observed overhead. Most of these plunged harmlessly into the sea, but one fell upon Molotea, completely destroying the eastern half of that atoll with the loss of seventy-three lives. American missile bases, situated mostly in Hawaii and the Philippines, waited for orders that never came, and speculated endlessly on the identity of the enemy. The last missile plunged into the sea, and no more came. The war was over, and the Old World had perished as completely as though it had never been.

Both Joenes and Lum were conscious but feeble during those days. The war was months past before they had regained their entire strength. But at last, each of them was ready to play his part in the shaping of the new civilization.

Sadly, they saw their duties in different ways, and were able to reach no substantial agreement. They tried to keep their friendship intact, but this became increasingly difficult. Their followers compounded the difficulties, and some thought that these two haters of war might start a war themselves.

But this was not to be. Joenes's influence in the South Pacific islands, from Nukuhiva in the west to Tongo in the east was predominant. Therefore Lum and his followers provisioned a number of canoes and sailed eastward, past Tonga to the Fijis, where Lum's ideas had excited considerable interest. They were both in middle age at this time, and they took leave of each other with genuine sorrow.

Lum's final words to Joenes were: "Well, man, I guess every cat has to find his own scene where he can swing. But frankly it bugs me going off this way, you know? You and I been through it, Joenesy, and we're the only ones who *know*. So even though I think you're wrong, keep punching in there, keed, and get the word across. I'm going to miss you, man, so take it easy."

Joenes expressed similar sentiments. Lum sailed to the Fijis, where his ideas found the greatest possible reception. Even today, Fiji is the centre of Lumism, and the Fijians do not speak the dialect of English derived from Joenes, but rather the dialect of English that Lum spoke. Some experts consider this to be the purest and most ancient form of the English language.

The most striking part of Lum's philosophy can be told in his own words, as written in the *Book of Fiji*:

Look, the whole thing happened in the way it happened on account of machines.
Machines are therefore bad. They are also made of metal. So metal is even worse. I mean it's evil.

So as soon as we get rid of all the damned metal, everything will swing.

This was only a part of Lum's teachings, of course. He
also had firm theories on the need for intoxication and
ecstatic joy ("You gotta swing"); about ideal behaviour
("Nobody oughta bug anybody"); about the limitations
societies should observe ("They shouldn't get on anybody's
back"); about the need for good manners, toleration, and
respect ("You shouldn't put nobody down"); about the importance of objectively determined sense-data ("I dig real
things the most"); about co-operation within a societal
framework ("It's pretty good when all the cats swing
together"); and many other things, covering nearly every
aspect of human life. These examples are taken from the
*Book of Fiji*, where all of Lum's sayings can be found complete with their annotations.

In those early days of the New World, the Fijians were
most interested in Lum's theory about the evil inherent in
metal. Being a naturally adventurous and far-travelling
people, they set sail in great fleets, led by Lum, to throw
metal into the sea wherever they could find it.

On their expeditions, the Fijians gathered new advocates
for the fiery Lumist faith. They spread the destruction of
metal throughout the Pacific, journeying past Australia to
the shores of the Americas. Their exploits are recorded in
numerous songs and stories, particularly of the work they
did in the Philippines, and, with the aid of the Maoris, in
New Zealand. Only late in the century, long after Lum's
death, were they able to complete their work in Hawaii,
thus ridding the Pacific Islands of an estimated nine-
tenths of their metal.

At the height of Fijian prestige, those fierce men briefly
conquered many of the islands they touched at. But they
were far too lacking in numbers to make their conquests

endure. For a while, Fijians ruled in Bora Bora, Raiatea, Huahine, and Oahu; but the local populations either absorbed them or drove them out. Also, most Fijians respected Lum's explicit instructions concerning islands other than the Fijis: "Do your bit and then split the scene; above all, do not hang around and be a party-poop."

Thus ended the Fijian adventure.

Joenes, unlike Lum, left behind no organized body of philosophical writings. He never explicitly disapproved of metal, but he was himself indifferent to it. He distrusted all laws, even the best, while at the same time recognizing the necessity for them. For Joenes, a law took its goodness from the nature of the men who administered it. When the nature if those men changed, as Joenes believed was inevitable, then the nature of the law changed, too. When this happened, new laws and new lawgivers had to be found.

Joenes taught that men should strive actively towards virtue, and at the same time recognize the extreme difficulties involved in that striving. The greatest of these difficulties, as Joenes saw it, was that all things, even men and their virtues, were continually changing, thereby forcing a lover of the good to abandon his illusions of permanence and to search out the changes occurring in himself and others, and to centre his goodness in a never-ending search for momentary stability in the midst of life's metamorphoses. On a quest like this, Joenes pointed out that one needed luck, which was indefinable but absolutely essential.

Joenes spoke of this and many other things, always stressing the excellence of virtue, the necessity for an active will, and the impossibility of perfection. Some say that in his old age Joenes preached in an entirely different way, and told men that the world was nothing more than a horrid toy built by evil gods; the form this toy took was that of a theatre, in which the gods put on endless plays for their own amusement, creating and using humans for the cast. And what the gods did was to stuff these men full of consciousness, and imbue this consciousness with virtues and ideals, hopes and dreams, and all manner of qualities and contradictions. Then, with the actors so constituted, the gods set problems for them, and found vast enjoyment in the spectacle of these strutting puppets, filled with their own importance, convinced of their place in the scheme of things, suspecting or proving their immortality, labouring to resolve the dilemmas the gods had put before them. The gods roared with laughter at this spectacle, and nothing delighted them more than to see some little puppet determined to live with decency and to die with dignity. The gods always applauded this, and laughed at the absurdity of death, the one thing that rendered all of man's solutions impossible. But even this was not the most terrible thing. In time, the gods would tire of their theatre and their little human puppets, would put them all away, tear down the theatre, and turn to other amusements. After a little while, not even the gods would remember that there had been men.

This tale is not characteristic of Joenes, and your editor does not think it worthy of him. We will always remember Joenes in the strength and pride of his middle years, when he preached a message of hope.

Joenes lived long enough to see the death of the old world and the birth of a new one. Today all civilization worthy of the name exists upon the islands of the Pacific. Our racial stock is mixed, and many of our ancestors came from Europe, America, or Asia. But for the most part we are Polynesian, Melanesian, and Micronesian. Your editor, who dwells upon the island of Havaiki, believes that our present peace and prosperity is a direct consequence of the smallness of our islands, their great number, and the large distances between them. This renders impossible any chance of total conquest by one group, and allows easy escape for any man who does not like his own island. These were advantages the people of the continents did not possess.

We have our difficulties, of course. Warfare still breaks out among the island groups, though on an infinitesimal scale in comparison to the wars of the past. There is still social inequality, injustice, crime, and disease; but these evils are never so great as to overwhelm the island societies. Life changes, and this change often seems to bring evil as well as progress; but the changes take place more slowly today than in the hectic past.

Perhaps this slowness of change is due in part to the great scarcity of metal. It was always in short supply in our islands, and the Fijians destroyed most of what was available. A little metal is sometimes dug out of the earth in the Philippines, but hardly any of it gets into circulation. Lumist societies are still active, and they steal any metal they can find and throw it into the sea. Many of us feel that this irrational hatred of metal is a deplorable thing; but we still cannot answer Lum's ancient question, with which the Lumists still taunt us.

The question goes: " Man, you ever try to build a atom bomb out of coral and coconut shells? "

This is how life is in the present day. With sadness we are forced to realize that our peace and prosperity rest upon the body of a ravaged society whose destruction made possible our existence. But this is the way of all societies, and there is nothing we can do about it. Some of the mourners of the past might do well to consider the future. Far-wandering bands of Fijian Lumists have reported a stir of movement in the savage tribes who now inhabit the continents. These scattered and fearful savages may be ignored for the moment; but who knows what the future will bring?

As for the end of the Journey, the following is told. Lum met his death at the age of sixty-nine. Leading a party of metal destroyers, Lum's head was stove in by the club of a huge Hawaiian who was trying to protect a sewing machine. Lum's final words were: "Well, boys, I'm on my way to that Big Tea Party in the Sky, run by the Greatest Junkie of them all."

So saying, he died. This was Lum's final recorded statement on religious matters.

With Joenes, the end came in an entirely different way. In his seventy-third year, while visiting the high island of Moorea, Joenes saw a disturbance on the beach and went down to see what was the matter. He found that a man of his own race had drifted ashore on a raft, his clothes in shreds and his limbs badly sunburned, but otherwise in good condition.

"Joenes!" the man cried. "I knew you were alive, and I was sure I'd find you. You are Joenes, aren't you?"

"I am," Joenes said. "But I'm afraid I don't recognize you."

"I'm Watts," the man said, "as in Watts the matter? I'm the jewel thief you met in New York. Do you remember me now?"

"Yes, I do," Joenes said. "But why have you sought me out?"

"Joenes, we talked for only a few moments, but you had a profound influence on me. Just as your Journey became your life, so *you* became my life. I cannot explain how this knowledge came to me, but it did come, and I found it irresistible. My work was you, and concerned only you. It was a long hard task for me to gather together everything you needed, but I did not mind. I received help, and marks of favour in high places, and was content. Then came the war, rendering everything more difficult. I had to wander for many years over the ravaged face of America to find what you would require, but I completed my work and came at last to California. From there I set sail for the islands of the Pacific, and for many years I went from place to place, often hearing of you, never finding you. But I never grew discouraged. I always remembered the difficulties *you* had to face, and took heart from them. I knew that your work had to do with the completion of a world; but my work had to do with the completion of *you*."

"This is very amazing," Joenes said in a calm voice. "I think perhaps you are not in complete possession of your senses, my dear Watts, but that makes no difference at all. I am sorry to have caused you so much trouble; but I had no idea you were looking for me."

"You could not know," Watts said. "Not even you, Joenes, could know who or what was looking for you until it found you."

"Well," Joenes said, "you have found me now. Did you say that you had something for me?"

"Several things," Watts said. "I have faithfully preserved and cherished them, since they are necessary for your completion."

Watts then took out an oilskin package that had been tied to his body. Smiling with pleasure, he handed the package to Joenes.

Joenes opened the package and found the following things:

1. A note from Sean Feinstein, who said that he had taken it upon himself to send these things, and also to provide Watts as an agent. He hoped that Joenes was well. As for himself, he had escaped the holocaust with his daughter Deirdre, and had gone to Sangar Island, two thousand miles off the coast of Chile. There he was enjoying a modest success as a trader, while Deirdre had married

an industrious and open-minded local boy. He sincerely hoped that these enclosures would be of value to Joenes.

2. A brief note from the doctor Joenes had met in the Hollis Home for the Criminally Insane. The doctor wrote that he remembered Joenes's interest in the patient who had believed himself to be God, and who had vanished before Joenes could meet him. However, since Joenes had been curious about the case, the doctor was enclosing the only bit of writing the madman had left—the list that had been found on his table.

3. A map of the Octagon marked with the official Cartographer's seal and approved by the highest officials. Marked "accurate and final" by the Chief of the Octagon himself. Guaranteed to take anyone to any part of the building, swiftly and without delay.

Joenes looked for a long time at these things, and his face became like weathered granite. For a long time he did not move, and then did so only when Watts tried to read the various papers over his shoulder.

"It's only fair!" Watts cried. "I carried them all this way, and I never looked at them. I must have one peek at that map, my dear Joenes, and just a glance at the madman's list."

"No," Joenes said. "These things weren't sent to you."

Watts became furiously angry, and the villagers had to restrain him from seizing the papers by force. Several of the village priests came expectantly up to Joenes, but he backed away from them. There was a look of horror on his face, and some people thought he would throw the papers into the sea. But he did not. He clutched them tightly to him and hurried up the steep trail into the mountains. The priests followed, but soon lost their way in the dense undergrowth.

They came down and told the people that Joenes would

soon return, and that he merely wished to study the papers alone for a while. The people waited and did not lose patience for many years, although Watts died. But Joenes never descended from the mountains.

Nearly two centuries later, a hunter climbed the high slopes of Moorea in search of wild goats. When he came down, he declared that he had seen a very old man sitting in front of a cave, looking at some papers. The old man had beckoned to him, and the hunter came forward, not without fear. He saw that the papers the old man held were faded by sun and rain to an indecipherable blur, and the old man himself seemed to have gone blind from reading them.

The hunter asked, "How can you read those papers?"

The old man answered, "I don't have to. I've learned them by heart."

Then the old man rose to his feet and went into the cave, and in a moment everything was as though he had never been.

Was this story true? In spite of his incredible age, could Joenes still be living in the mountains and thinking about the highest secrets of a vanished age? If so, did the madman's list and the Octagon map have any meaning for our own age?

We will never know. Three expeditions to the place have turned up no evidence of human habitation, although the cave is there. Scholars believe that the hunter must have been drunk. They reason that Joenes went out of his mind with grief at receiving important information too late; that he fled from the priests and dwelt like a hermit with his fading and useless papers; and finally died in some inaccessible place.

This explanation seems only reasonable; but the people of Moorea have built a small shrine on the site.

No. 1   KURT VONNEGUT

### The Sirens of Titan

"A classic, ripe with wit and eloquence and a
cascade of inventiveness" – Brian Aldiss
0 575 03819 5

No. 2   THEODORE STURGEON

### More Than Human

Winner of the International Fantasy Award
"A masterpiece" – James Blish
0 575 03821 7

No. 3   ROBERT SILVERBERG

### A Time of Changes

Winner of the Nebula Award
"Highly recommended" – *TLS*
0 575 03820 9

No. 4   SAMUEL R. DELANY

### Nova

"His rampaging talent mesmerises the reader" –
*Tribune*
0 575 03818 7

No. 5   ARTHUR C. CLARKE

### The City and the Stars

"One of the most imaginative novels of the
very far future ever written" – *Sunday Times*
0 575 03849 7

No. 6   ROBERT A. HEINLEIN

**The Door into Summer**

"Highly readable" – *Punch*

0 575 03850 0


No. 7   FREDERIK POHL &
C. M. KORNBLUTH

**Wolfbane**

"A work of sheer, exuberant imagination" –
Arthur C. Clarke

0 575 03852 7


No. 8   JOHN SLADEK

**The Reproductive System**

"Superb entertainment . . . full of invention, wit
and subtly sad comedy" – *Sunday Times*

0 575 03851 9


No. 9   ARTHUR C. CLARKE

**A Fall of Moondust**

"The best book Arthur C. Clarke has done" –
John Wyndham

0 575 03978 7


No. 10   BOB SHAW

**A Wreath of Stars**

"Staggeringly enjoyable . . . It wouldn't put
me down" – Brian Aldiss

0 575 03980 9

No. 11   ALGIS BUDRYS

**Rogue Moon**

"A masterpiece" – James Blish
0 575 03979 5

No. 12   FREDERIK POHL

**Man Plus**

"A soaring monument to mankind's folly,
pettiness and ultimate glory" – *The Times*
0 575 03981 7

No. 13   CHRISTOPHER PRIEST

**Inverted World**

"A spinning originality grips every page"
– *Listener*
0 575 03993 0

No. 14   DANIEL KEYES

**Flowers for Algernon**

"A narrative *tour-de-force*" –
*Science Fiction: the 100 Best Novels*
0 575 04061 0

No. 15   ROBERT SHECKLEY

**Journey Beyond Tomorrow**

"Robert Sheckley is the greatest entertainer
ever produced by modern science fiction" – J.G. Ballard
0 575 04122 6

No. 16   HARLAN ELLISON (ed)

## Dangerous Visions

"You will find here the field at its most
experimental and daring" – Isaac Asimov

0 575 04144 7

*Available from October 1987*

No. 17   SAMUEL R. DELANY

## Babel–17

"Hits you like a magnesium flare at
midnight" – *Tribune*

0 575 04123 4

No. 18   FREDERIK POHL &
C.M. KORNBLUTH

## Gladiator-at-Law

"Frighteningly convincing: how well
these two write" – *Daily Telegraph*

0 575 04127 7